by L E Fryer-Stokes

65: Stage One – The Phone Call

It started with a Tuesday as I was polishing the barrel of my Glock, a prerequisite for absolutely anyone in my line of work. Powerful and reliable, the .45 GAP can be extremely accurate when placed in the right hands, though most of my work these days involves the Parker-Hale and calls less and less for the Glock. It is a pity, because the Glock and I share more of an understanding than I do with any of my rifles. I suppose it is because the rifles are designed to be used anonymously, from a distance, when The Target poses no threat to me – does not, in fact, ever see my face – whereas the Glock has always been more of a personal bodyguard, almost a friend. Often in the past the GAP has been all that has stood between me and Death. I owe it many things, so to clean it once a week seems like the least I can do.

I was running the bore brush in and out of the barrel, and philosophising – as one tends to do when one reaches this indecisive middle age – and in my philosophising, stumbled upon the answer to a question that has plagued mankind for all the ages since the very first ape concluded that scratching your bottom with both hands whilst swinging from a tree is probably *not* the most intelligent course of action in the history of evolution; and then, whilst nursing a sore backside, made fire.

I digress. My concentration is not what it used to be; so many different people come in and out of my life so continuously that I hardly get a moment to myself to reflect. Though, in the rare moments when I do have time to myself, rather than reflect I tend to reach for my Glock and clean it, perhaps to take my mind off the possibility that I might have to sit down and reflect. It is a vicious cycle.

More vicious still is the undeserved brutality with which my loyal companion finally turned its back on me, as if to say, *Your gunning days are numbered, my friend; find a new hobby.*

It was unexpected, but I suppose I was more than partly to blame, because it was the shock of realising I had just had an epiphany that momentarily stole my attention away, and when one is cleaning guns – or doing anything with guns, for that matter – one should be aware that even the slightest lapse in concentration can result in the most dreadful miscalculations, and put holes in places where holes are honestly not wanted.

I particularly and especially wanted no hole in any one of my limbs.

Yes, I openly admit that the blame is entirely mine. It can hardly be said that the GAP did this thing of its own accord. No matter the leaps in technology that might bring about sentience in ordinary household objects, my GAP is an old model and not given to spontaneously shooting me.

It took me a few seconds to register the sound of the shot, and my first thought, as it might have been, was not, 'Dammit, I've shot myself!'

It was not even 'Somebody's shooting! Duck and cover!' as it would have been at an earlier stage in my life, when training was fresh in my mind and I walked about on drawing pins and broken glass.

I suppose it *should* have been, 'Where did the bullet go?' or 'I hope no-one heard that', and not 'What have I left in the microwave?', as it actually was.

Accompanied by a burning smell, this microwave theory seemed the most plausible at the time.

Only when the warmth started spreading between my toes, as if I had just stepped, socks and all, into a bucket of caramel, did I chance a look down, and then and there come to the conclusion that I had not left anything in the microwave, but rather done the unthinkable, and shot a hole in my foot.

Ouch.

I can't walk right now, but hopping is a good enough way of getting from place to place.

I hop to the kettle and make myself a cup of tea. Milk, one sugar, and rather a lot of soluble morphine – just in case, when the adrenaline wears off, I find that the experience of shooting oneself is actually quite painful.

Oops… Just fell over. Don't remember kitchen being this uneven. Maybe have mole problem. Wait…live on seventh floor…

~

When I woke it was light. I'd crawled onto the sofa and draped myself with a towel, and somewhere between shooting myself and losing consciousness must have tried to sew up the bullet-hole.

It's actually quite neat work, to say that I don't remember anything of it, though it will have to be redone. I last remember seeing that particular purple ball of wool at the bottom of my wardrobe, and this surely can't make for the cleanest sutures.

I received The Call as I was with sticky fingers attempting to thread a very fine needle, and The Voice on the end of the line made me drop and lose the needle in the carpet. I listened in the customary silence.

In preparation for Mission 65, I am to devise a new identity, drill it into my brain and tuck away my real self so that not even the most professional professional can extract and torture it; and all this by Friday. Goodness knows how I'm to find time to do all this, and still get to the bottom of the ironing pile. Such is the demanding nature of life, I suppose, although it can hardly be said that death is any less taxing.

~

My name is Jeremiah. I live in a hackneyed apartment, from which I can see maple trees and graffiti. I have a black cat named Sodom. I've had a few cats, actually, Sodom all. I clean windows in my spare time, putting the money towards the expansion of my prize-winning paper-clip collection. I'm a telemarketer, at least until my dreams take off. I want to be a florist, though goodness knows where that interest came from. I've never wanted to be a florist before in all my days.

My father died whilst doing his duty to God. By that I mean he was handling the dean's assets during an Interregnum when a 15th-century bronze crucifix shrugged off its Jesus and the twelve tonne Son of God flattened him like a pancake.

My mother has since remarried and is living in Wellington with a Mexican named Fernandez. I would like to do terrible things to Fernandez with a grapefruit spoon.

My name is Jeremiah-Joseph. My friends call me JJ. Jay. Jerry. I eat mayonnaise from a spoon, straight out of the jar. I have a drinking problem but am otherwise comfortable with my own sexuality.

~

I just found the needle I dropped earlier and I'm now removing it from my heel. The same heel belonging to the foot I shot. Not a good day for my left foot.

After receiving The Call, I came to realise that I have reached a milestone; this will be my sixty-fifth assignment. Perhaps I should mark the occasion with a bottle of claret. Actually, I despise claret. Perhaps a fine Merlot. What goes with chicken?

No – I will wait until my seventieth assignment and celebrate that. If I am still alive by then. Danger goes with the territory in my line of work. Death is always waiting *just* around the corner. Sometimes he follows me, too.

THEY will phone again tomorrow, at *exactly* thirty-seven minutes and eighteen seconds past four. I will learn about The Target, the bare facts. *Age, weight, height, appearance, shoe size.* No names – never any names. Thing are simple when there are no names.

Only, there was a name, the last time.

A face, pale as daisy chains. Hair like broken biscuits. White cotton dress stained with fading lilies. White heels, stained with fading years. No names, until I pulled the trigger. Bullet slid through soft wet flesh, a thousand miles an hour, angled down like Cupid's arrow to punch through her heart…

She didn't cry out, only opened her mouth and framed a sorrow no years of training can teach us to erase. And her girlfriend screamed, and cried her name, and Jennifer stained my heart forever, like the blood that can't be drilled out of the pavement.

I never knew a girl called Jennifer. I never knew a girl whose name rang of worn-down heels and red-hooped ears, who chewed her gum with a slack jaw and walked with a wiggle and who didn't scream as the bullet clawed into her heart.

I never knew a girl called Jennifer. I never knew her dying thoughts. But I saw her dying eyes, looked right at them down my scope, and I knew a girl who didn't want to die, but could feel the soft pull of Death, and could not wriggle free, nor jam her high white heel into his groin.

I saw Jennifer die without a word.

I think I will retire to bed now and find out more of Jeremiah's hobbies. They must not too closely resemble my own.

65: Stage Two – The Target

It is raining. The rain is falling on my face. A few drops drip from a crack in the ceiling where damp has spread in fuzzy patches that make the peeling plaster weave and yip like a pack of Dalmatians.

I wake with a jolt, thinking I am back in China. The room was four feet by four feet and I couldn't stand straight without hitting my head. There were no leaks in that room, though; the drips come later, when you hang by your toes from a hook.

I thought about Jeremiah last night. Talked to him, learned his secrets. He is tall, tanned, with long fingers that play piano music even when they're still. He has dark hair, short and curling. Light brown eyes that smile and speak of days on the sands of Goa, or watching the sunset over the sunken city of Venice.

He is a likeable guy, as it happens. A good listener. He knows how to say *just* the right things, no matter the company. The women watch him from the corner of their eyes, looking at his long fingers and his long legs and his long nose, and smile at his soft eyes and watch the way he walks, and wonder if he has a girlfriend, or a wife, but see something in his white-dove smile that looks like freedom.

He drinks iced coffee and banana milkshakes. He has his tuna-cucumber on white bread, with plenty of mayonnaise, and only eats the crust on one side.

He eats Mars Bars in twos and doesn't know anything about gambling, but knows *exactly* how to talk about it, as if he's done it all his life. He only reads the newspaper if the headlines are good, only buys shirts on sale, never eats the liquorice from his Sherbet Fountain.

He hates Saturdays, to my despair. They are lazy days, days without purpose, and Jeremiah is a purposeful man.

He likes the old black-and-whites at the cinema, but for some reason he just can't stomach theatre. And he *hates* Marmite, and he never drinks the last inch of orange juice.

He tried dog once, in Singapore, and was violently ill for three days; could not look a dog in the eyes afterwards; pledged £400 in one go to Labrador Lifeline, to try and appease his guilt.

The smell of Jack Daniel's makes him ill; the sight of blood makes him faint; yet death has never scared him.

I'm sure he's not all good, though. No-one's all good. He'll show me his dark side sooner or later.

Sooner or later, everyone does.

~

The Target is a man, this time. I received The Call at thirty-seven minutes and eleven seconds past four (it seems my clock is slow), and held onto silence as the words spiralled down the line and spilled like warm castor oil into my ear.

The Target is a man. The man is sixty-one years old. He has a paunch and is not a tall man, but he looks over the heads of those he passes, and through their eyes, and does not see the human beings whose dignity he offends. He thinks it is dog mess his size nine Italian loafers step in, but it is the hurt of those he disregards, those he runs down, those he looks beyond as if they were glass walls through which blood and love and pain did not flow.

He walks beneath a perpetually clear sky, but it's one he has bought, because he has the money to buy anything and everything, and anyone. Because he has never felt a pleasure he hasn't paid for.

I walked across to the park after The Call, and sat on a bench.

In memory of Jeanie Andrews,
who we will love and remember forever

I never knew a Jeanie before, but I sat on her bench and felt her sun-warmed wood caress my cloth-clad thighs.

Sun spat through the false acacias above and behind me, tickling my neck's back with warm and cool, dancing with a hush-hush secrecy in the Springy breeze, laughing softly at the children playing loud ball by the rotten metal goal-posts.

Jeremiah played ball when he was a boy, by a lake on which ducks swam and swans preened, on which the wind danced and made itself seen, on which the bloody autumn leaves dripped as the stormy winter sky roiled by overhead.

The vicious winds ripped roads through the trees and buffeted the absent-minded boys who, in their t-shirts and shorts, had not noticed the passing of summer, the onset of snow.

I have never played ball. I have no childhood, not one I can recall. I had no birthday parties in darkened rooms, with tiny candles sputtering in the gloom. I had no friends to eat.

It was dark when I returned, hungry. Hungry, but too tired to make omelette. I compiled a cheese sandwich, thickly spread with Marmite, and settled down at my desk to study The Files.

The Mission Files. Manila folders with red elastic bindings, numbered one to sixty-five in big, black, bold letters. Permanent letters; permanent scars.

Each File is packed with dog-eared papers, finger-printed photographs, handwritten notes, sticky sweet wrappers. Chocolate, fudge, caramel, nougat, crème, sweat, blood. Gold wrappers, green foil, purple paper. Sherbet-smeared orange tubes, discarded liquorice strands.

Folder sixty-five was empty, as all the other folders should have been. They should not even exist, in fact, but I can never find the heart to burn them, to erase the memory of each Mission I have completed, each Target I have terminated.

I flicked through them, picking random numbers and opening the manila binders to find a familiar face. I knew almost nothing of these people, but everything of their faces. I knew their eyes. I could read their eyes as well as any map.

My foot is a little better today, though I still have a limp. As I left the building to sit in the park, the kids on the corner (oblivious to Death) pointed and mocked, 'Hobbling Henry, Hobbling Henry'. I ignored them and hurried across the road, but every fibre of my soul remembered Max and *he* wanted to cut their hearts out.

I've never even known a Henry, let alone been one. I was Harry, once. Harry was allergic to strawberries and hated the colour orange because once when he was six his mother threw an orange at his father and told him to *fuck off*, and the orange broke against the wall and sprayed Harry with orange blood. Harry's favourite colour was blue.

I've been Mickey, who had a hamster called Marbles and buried it alive. He hadn't meant to, but he thought it was dead when it was really only hibernating and it dug its way out of the grave. Mickey screamed like a little girl when he found the tiny tunnel of Marbles' escape.

I've been Ned, who knocked a pan of boiling water off the stove when he was four and burned himself down both legs, and whose mother could only grunt and roll over and spill her whisky as he cried. The scars were there forever, they never went away. His mother died at thirty-five, when Ned was just fifteen; he didn't cry.

I've been Robert, a genius at maths, a lost cause at life. I've been Jack, the harmless druggie, the joker, the idiot. I've been Gerald, who hated all the world and still dreamt of being the first man on the moon.

I've been Eric who lived next door and seemed alright, but who had an axe in the cupboard under his sink and had never chopped wood in his life.

And I've been Max. Max, whose short blonde hair stood up without prompt, whose bright blue eyes looked green in the sunlight. Max, whose background was a blur of foster homes and foster families, whose confidence stemmed from the knowledge that he had been tested and he had survived. Max, whose temper was a calm ocean and a raging tempest, whose charms were ingrained and whose job was to die for. Maximillian, whose name was a great number, whose name was a gangster, whose name was a power with which to be reckoned. Whose name could influence the outcome of revolutions.

Something about Max reminded me of Jeremiah, though not so tall and not so dark. And he smoked. And sometimes he stormed, while Jeremiah was mostly quiet. A shadow, a wraith, Jeremiah didn't like to make waves. Maximillian was the hand of an angry god, and he made tsunami.

A sheet of crisp white ice slid through my fax machine. There was ink on the ice, bleeding.

It bled into the shape of a man's face.

A sixty-one-year-old man whose bloated gut was solid with the gold he swallowed whole. I stared long and hard at that man's jowled face, traced the outline of his small nose with the worn-down rubber of my pencil. Tapped the sharpened lead against the whites of his sightless eyes.

13

Then I pushed the image into my mind and pushed the paper into The File.

~

I fell asleep before my bedtime and dreamed. I dreamed of Holland and windmills over water. I dreamed I was on a barge, smoking pipe tobacco, one hand on the wheel, a green hat on my head. I dreamed I lost my hat to the four winds, and it fell into the water and was eaten by a shark.

I've never been to Holland, I thought, as I woke in the dark.

It seemed pointless to sleep again, so I rose and stared about me through the gloom. Stared at the cubicle where I have come to live. Stared at the stain on the lino, the tiny bullet-hole through which I had popped a Cupid's arrow and part of my foot. I wonder only now where the bullet went.

I don't remember when I came here, but I remember tearing down the orange curtains and replacing them with blue. I remember another bullet-hole, gaping like a blinded eye, staring at me from the wall where I had shot it when the lights went out, and all that was left was the darkness and the fire and the Glock in my hand, and I remember hanging the painting over it, and hating the painting, and being too frightened to pull it down, in case the bullet-hole could somehow suck me back into that dark world, where nothing existed but me and my pain.

The painting is the only one to have been hung. Its frame is plagued by gilt, the picture itself indescribably horrific. I buy plants, sometimes, when the mood for living things takes hold of me; placed within the immediate vicinity of the loathed painting, these victims die immediately. Placed within a five-metre radius, they suffer slowly and are but shadows before the week is out.

The painting is Hiroshima, the painting is Nagasaki, the painting is death on a radiating scale. It covers a pit that has drilled deeper than the superficial plaster, scarring the very soul of this cubicle where Death itself resides.

In my kitchen there is a kettle. It is an object of lust, an object of comfort, a source of warmth and healing around which much of my life revolves. It is a friend in lonely hours. My only friend, besides the Glock.

Perhaps I have let these household objects take on too much life, become almost sentient. But it will be worth it, if one day they make me tea before I wake, or fire a shot to save my life without having to be asked.

Outside it is dark. Darker than bubbling pitch and twice as thick. The bubbles rise slowly and in silence, breaking only as they reach the surface to release the sounds they have collected from the murky world below. The rev and squeal and honk of cars, the click of heels, the screech of voices. The buzz of lights that line the roads, the hum of roads beyond the lights.

The soundless sound of night, when crickets in some distant patch of grass chirrup and electrify the air. The birds are quiet. Perhaps at night they fall asleep, or die.

I lift the window. The night air is treacle, warm with tar and tyres. I breathe it in and feel no rush of life.

The window shut, the curtains pulled, I slip back to the silence of my room.

65: Stage Three – Becoming Jeremiah

I rise with the sun most mornings. I am up with the birds that sing from the eaves far above me. I seek solace from my nightmares in the kettle, and drink hot tea as I eat my toast and watch the city wake. I have peanut butter when I have dreamed of flight; Marmite when I am too tired to wake; marmalade to appease the hungry cat when I had overslept, or jam to appease the sun, who is invariably angry that I have missed a single moment of his birth, and shucks a coat of clouds across his face. This morning it is peanut butter.

I often dream of flying, though I have never flown. In dreams I only fly when no-one's looking, for if they see me I crash to the ground and can fly no more. I dream that I am flying through a sky of cloudless blue, and that if I spread my wings I can fly all the way to the moon. I have never been to the moon before.

Today there will be no Call. Today THEY will be silent, and I will be allowed to think about The Target and become Jeremiah. I must know Jeremiah's every thought, as I must know my Target inside and out.

At *precisely* seventeen minutes past two this afternoon I will receive another Fax. This will be *exactly* four pages long and will contain information vital to my comfortable acquaintance with The Target. But I will have no information on Jeremiah.

I rifle through my clothes-boxes and find an outfit he would like. Long-legged jeans, a cream sweater, a pale blue shirt. Brown shoes, not smart, unpolished. I realise he carries a handkerchief embroidered with JJR, and a tiny A-Z from somewhere only he has been.

Though it is a bright day, Jeremiah will not wear shades. Not like Max – Max lived in shades, as though to keep from shaming the beautiful sky with his beautiful eyes. Max had no need for a map. He knew his way anywhere, even as a stranger. Max never got lost. Max never made mistakes.

I leave the apartment with Jeremiah, and see where he wants to take me.

~

Jeremiah walks without thinking where he places his feet. He avoids cracks in the pavement instinctively and steps carefully over the lines of ants that cross his path, bearing loads far heavier than themselves. Jeremiah respects the ants. They are hard-working, honest folk.

We move aside as someone comes our way and does not wish to alter their trajectory. We sidestep and often end up in the gutter if a woman wants to pass. We hold open doors that jingle for ladies who jangle with jewels and who give us smiles that do not reach the eyes that weigh us up.

We smile back, pretending we are comfortable being naked before their judgemental, animal gaze. Jeremiah is comfortable. Max and I are not.

I cannot help but compare Max and Jeremiah. The very way they walk and stand sets them apart like animals of the jungle. Jeremiah is a giraffe, tall and gentle and docile. He browses through the leaves and takes his pick of the best, but is still kind to those he chooses not to eat, brushing softly against them as if to say *I hold you in no lower regard that those I chose to eat. I simply did not eat you.* It does not seem possible that he could be a killer.

Max, with his wild hair and all-seeing eyes, is a lion. He prowls the streets of life and those around him feel his presence as a soft rustling, like the warm breeze across an African plain, and it sends shivers through their bodies.

They are his prey, the women and the men; they know they can walk safely past him only as long as he is sated and at rest. For when he is hungry, he strikes out for one of them and sinks in his teeth, so loving a caress that it does not seem like death. It is sweet, soft, satisfying. It is a gesture that those who have escaped him actually long for, and those who are his victims feel honoured to receive.

Jeremiah takes me to a newsagent, a tiny dusty place protected by a faded awning, beneath which stalls of faded fruits dry and wither in the faded sun.

Inside it is an ancient library, the shelves stacked with tins and bars and packets and cartons whose letters read like poetry in the dancing motes of sunlight.

I want to buy a bag of Maltesers and a bottle of juice. Jeremiah reaches for a salad sandwich, sees the soggy bread and replaces it with care. I want a paper to read as we sit outside the café we will visit next. He buys a raspberry smoothie and two Mars Bars, then we leave.

We go to the café. He flicks idly through the A-Z as we eat the café's salmon and cucumber baguette, and drink the smoothie, and pick delicately over a slice of carrot cake. There's nothing in that book he needs to know; he just likes to have something to do with his hands. And it's useful as a conversation starter, though no-one bites the bait today. He orders an iced coffee, with cream.

The sun is at its African peak, hot against our skin. Jeremiah tans easily, his brown eyes taking on a hazel tinge. I am already beginning to burn. The skin beneath Jeremiah's is my own, and he lets the sunlight through to scald my face, my arms, my hands.

We read on, soaking in each soggy word and swelling like a sponge. Warm, swollen and content, we leave the crust of the baguette and the last inch of the iced coffee and are gone before the waitress teeters past to tidy up the corpse of our meal, and Jeremiah's generous tip.

Though it is only just midday, the city is bathed with soft pink-golden light. The park glints wetly and with promise as we return home, hushing sleepily in its leaves. We cross the street with ease and care, and find the bench that remembers Jeanie Andrews.

It is occupied. A woman with a pram is resting on its sun-warmed wood, rocking the baby gently with her foot. She looks up as we pass and Jeremiah smiles at her, then at the baby. Before I can beckon him on, he stops by the pram and holds out a long finger. I am frozen, a deer caught in the headlights of its death. The baby has clutched our finger in its tiny chubby hand, and is squeezing with remarkable strength for something so small. Its eyes are huge in its fat little head. It is the night-monkey, nocturnal eyes staring at us from the highest branches of Jeremiah's chosen tree.

Beautiful baby, I hear Jeremiah say, as he sits down for a moment beside the woman, finger still in the grips of the chubby night-monkey. He talks to her for a while, but I am speechless and lost in the baby's brilliant stare. It has perfected the art of entrapment. It has lured me in. Will it devour me? It is but six months old, and already it knows all the secrets of the world. It knows Death, for it has survived the hardest journey of its youth. It knows life, for it has suckled at the teat through which life flows. It knows grief, and love, for it is loved when it cries and brought to silence by the knowledge it is loved.

And it knows me, for I am all these things; death, life, grief and love. It knows me to my very soul.

Very soon we leave, extricating ourselves from the mother and the night-monkey, and find another bench on the other side of the lake. This faces the apartment where I spend the hours of my existence; where we suffer in silence and see the world only through glass.

I stare at my apartment and see nothing. Jeremiah stares and sees the place where he was born.

I scan the windows of the surrounding cubicles and find a familiar face.

There is an elderly man who lives downstairs, two flats beneath and one to the left of my own. He is a sour man who lives his lonely life in silence, answering the door only to make the knocking stop.

He has seen too much of the world, and loved too little. He has been hurt by disappointment and is disappointed by his pain, for it did not bring the release it promised and so he must linger on, as he has done all his life.

He sits by the window as we watch him, and stares hatefully at the children playing in the park. He hates their noise because he has grown accustomed to the silence in which he must decay, and he dislikes change.

He hates the laughter that drifts up and batters his window because it reminds him that he does not know how to laugh, or has forgotten, and cannot remember the last time any sound left his lips besides grumbles or groans.

But he does not hate the children.

He does not hate them, because he wishes he could run with them and reclaim the childhood poverty and war stole away.

He wishes he could know the joy of being free, and run once more on legs he lost for a country those children neither respect nor wish to know.

Jeremiah is a good talker. As I watch the watcher, he tells me of his childhood on a farm. The farm had a pond to which he lost many a good football, as well as a brother when Jeremiah was just a baby.

He had a sister, Adelheid, older by two years. They strayed far from the parish when they were young, climbing the foothills of the mountains that encased the valley in which they lived. They chased goats and waded barefoot in streams, finding tiny nooks and caves across the front of which they built great doors from rocks and sticks and moss, and sat inside the damp, echoing silence for hours, listening to each other breathe and scratching one another's legs with their bare toes. When the danger outside had passed they would emerge, and race each other down into the valley, through the long grasses, grabbing at the wheat-like heads, pulling them off and scattering them to the winds.

When he was nineteen he moved to the city, bored with life as a preacher's son. He got a job as a clerk, shared a flat with three boys; Andrew was a student, Michael a trainee chef, Simon a DJ who worked in a record shop during the day. They liked Jeremiah well enough, and he they, but something about him remained mysterious to them, and they found they could not bond over beers as they would like. He moved out after six months and quit his job to half-heartedly study environmental conservation. He volunteered in a library, spending most of his time reading poetry in the back sections as he pretended to sort the books.

At college he was the basketball team's pride and joy, but only because he was tall and could shoot, or lose with grace. When his team won, Jeremiah watched them celebrate. They never excluded him, but he could not bring himself to be involved.

He didn't judge them – well, maybe he did, but only a little – but what kept him separate was the fact that his height and calm manner and permanent half-smile made him seem aloof, and the faith he had learned from his father made him feel that he should try to be better than those drunken revellers clashing beer glasses and head-butting each other in jest. He didn't mean to *think* that he was better than them; he only wanted to try to be a better person. But somehow that equated to the same thing.

We headed home as the sun grew cold. I cooked courgette and pineapple soufflé, but Jeremiah didn't stay to taste it. He took a sundae spoon of mayonnaise to suck on, delicately, and left when I saw the four-page Fax hanging from the machine's slitted mouth.

The time on the top corner reads 2.19pm (I really must check my clocks) and The Fax details The Target's life – everything from education to arrest warrants issued, of which there are none. But that means nothing, of course. The best ones pay to have such things expunged from any record of their lives – not through shame, but out of pride and vanity. Once I have finished reading, I muse, no doubt the other deadly sins will be revealed, too.

The Fax reads like an obituary, which I suppose it is. It is a tribute to a high-flyer, a real achiever, a man who has made more money in his career than I have in mine, though has killed fewer people to attain it. In a literal sense, he has killed no-one, but in every other sense he is a murderer of hearts; a shark of the business world, slaying competitors and colleagues with equal abandon; a habitual womaniser, cheating repeatedly on his wife with her knowledge and without her forgiveness.

His concessions to charity are attempts to balance out the selfishness he displays in every other aspect of his life – the expensive cars he doesn't drive, the expensive clothes, the expensive drinks, the expensive hotel stays with women he spoils more lavishly than his wife, if only because he has to buy their affections, whilst she loves him for nothing.

Three children at private schools; a house in Vermont; a yacht. I am not a jealous person, and I don't envy his wealth. But it is not often I find it easy to dislike a Target. Mostly you have to learn to read between the lines, to see what isn't written in The Files. To invent a person you have never met nor will ever see, until you are looking at them through the sights of your Russian Dragunov. I learned that skill a long time ago, after years of seeing paper good guys turn to bad guys in the flesh. This one makes it easy; I dislike this one without trying.

There was a knock at my door. I froze, blood like ice water. When I started toward the source of the sound, the Glock was already where it belonged.

I listened for a moment, standing in darkness by the door – not in front, never in front. I could hear breathing on the other side, soft and slow. I closed my eyes, listened to the breathing. The sounds of nighttime outside faded. Those breaths were like waves rolling up a beach, shushing over the sand, rhythmically retreating and returning. Beneath them, the gentle, liquid thud-thud of a nervous heartbeat.

I waited a moment longer, until she raised her hand to knock again, then opened the door. I had already holstered the Glock.

"Oh, er, hi," she falters softly. "We haven't really met, have we? I'm the girl downstairs."

I smile, ask how she is, concealing a nervousness that jumps up and down my spine like electricity, shivering through my limbs. I fold my arms to hide the fact my fingers are twitching.

"How…are you?" she asks.

I smile again and nod, steeling myself for the usual inane small-talk. Already I wish she would leave; already I wonder if she will stay.

"I…I just came up…to ask if you…if…" She puts her arms around her ribcage and bends one leg outward a little, tilting her head up and searching for the words that won't come. "I just came to ask…if you were okay. After, you know…" She sighs. "Look, you shot a hole in my ceiling."

Ah. The shot.

I apologise.

She stares at me. "What? Look, I don't know what you're doing with a gun, but you could have got someone killed…"

I smile and tell her it wasn't a gun, though she could be mistaken for thinking it was.

"Er, then…what was it?"

I explain that I was trying to open a bottle of Jacob's Creek Chardonnay that had obviously been shaken up a bit on its way back from Sainsbury's, and all the compressed CO_2 inside had forced the cork out with such vigour that it had punched right through the floor.

She raises an eyebrow, briefly, disbelievingly, and folds her arms defensively across her chest. I continue to smile, willing her to believe my lies.

Eventually she leaves, glancing back over her shoulder at me as if to check that I'm not tracing her with a scope. Not that she could know I have a scope.

Stupid fool! I should have been more careful.

Maybe I should take her out… But that requires clearance and paperwork, and a lot of unnecessary mess.

Once I'd shut the door, I rested back against the spattered beige walls and felt something in my chest shudder and heave. I was sweating profusely, shaking at the hands, and made more nervous by the girl downstairs than I'd ever felt in Geneva.

65: Stage Four – Tracing the Target

Max didn't do mornings. Max was a party animal, lazy until the sun was fully at its zenith. He would snore loudly and absently into his pillow until the honk of lunchtime traffic pulled him from between the sheets, then would languish in the bath for an interminable stretch before emerging to down triple shots of coffee, full-fat bacon rashers, and pretzels smothered in cheese.

Jeremiah likes mornings. He yawns and stretches and gets me from my bed just as dawn breaks jaggedly through the horizon. He watches the sun until it has risen, musing on his dreams and wondering what the rest of the city is doing, then insists on doing stretches before squeezing some oranges and sucking down the juice.

Wincing from the pain of tender calf muscles, I wonder how he and Harry would get along. Probably not well.

Leaving Jeremiah to his philosophical aerobics, I climbed onto the kitchen work-surface and pulled my M-85 down from the top of the cupboard. Hidden beneath the black velvet folds, inside what innocuously appears to be a trumpet case, is my Parker-Hale .308 M-85 sniper rifle.

I pulled the gun and its various necessary parts – detachable bi-pod, telescopic sights – from the case, and began assembly. Slowly at first, becoming accustomed to the rifle after having spent the last nineteen days with only my Glock for company.

The previous Mission, number sixty-four, was Simon's Mission, and Sim preferred the T-76 Dakota Longbow, which is capable of hitting a Target almost a mile away. That was a difficult shot for Sim to make, though not as difficult as Niall's shot. Niall also liked the Longbow; liked the name more than anything. He was the one who shot Jennifer – Jennifer who didn't cry. Sometimes I forget who shot her, but it was definitely Niall.

I disassemble the Parker-Hale – Max would have called it the M-85, but I don't, because that makes it sound like a motorway, and Jeremiah *loathes* traffic – and reassemble it again, as fast as I can. The metal is cold, comfortable and familiar in my hands. My fingers tingle along the slender barrel to the sound of shingle, remembering each firm caress of the trigger that sent a bullet down its length to plant a full stop at the end of a Target's book of breaths.

Once finished with the Parker-Hale, I wash my hands and hair. Short, light brown, it could curl at a moment's notice or lighten in the sun to Max's blond mane.

The bathroom is clean, neat, ordered. Everything is in its place now that Max has gone. The bottles rank neatly on the shelves, the sponge hangs at ease from a hook. Toothpaste and toothbrush are banded together with elastic. The soap no longer promises to trip me as I walk past the open shower door. But it is *too* orderly now that Jeremiah has moved in.

Every container faces front so its label is visible; the towels are folded in perfect right-angles over the handrail. I can picture Max wrinkling his nose at the scene, as though detecting an unpleasant odour. The odour of order, the scent of another creature marking its territory.

Part of me wonders where Max went. His was Mission 22, back in the early days. Not so early that he didn't know what he was doing, but early enough that he didn't care if things got a little sloppy. Just so long as the end result was neat. He messed around, but he never missed.

There have been others – Ned, Harry, Paulston, Daryl, Robert, Barry, Mickey, Edward, Gerald, Eric, Ben, Christoph, Marcus, Simon, Shaun, to name but a few – but unlike each of these, who take on only one Mission, then disappear forever, Max and I have faced a total of seven Missions together. It is unusual, and I am told *never* to work with the same shooter twice. But he keeps coming back, and won't take a hint. He thinks he can do the job when others can't.

He thinks I need him.

I scratch the thin layer of stubble shadowing my jaw. Jeremiah prefers neatness, so I switch on the mirror light to shave by. The fuse blows and takes all the other lights with it, leaving the apartment in a state of early dawn gloom.

Great. Now I must piss in the dark.

~

Morning comes hot and bubbling. There will be a Call in the early afternoon, though this is never made at the same time twice. This will tell me where to encounter The Target and I will have less than an hour to reach the location and set everything up.

I receive The Call at forty three minutes past one (very gratefully, for Jeremiah has me trying yoga and I am bent into the most uncomfortable shapes) and I'm given the time, location, distance from Target, the wind direction and speed, the number of people estimated to be in the vicinity at the time.

I wait by the door, Glock cocked and raised, as The Key rattles onto my mat.

65: Stage Five – Taking The Shot

Mason Road Hotel, Room 65

The room is old cigarettes. Bleak. Blinded by yellowing shades that are meant to fill the air with cheery light, but miss the target utterly and shoot at dreary instead. The dust-filtered sunlight turns the ageing bed-sheets grey. Cheap, unimaginative paintings trip over each other across the walls.

I tilt the blinds just enough to slip a muzzle between the slats and hook one finger to crack the window and banish the stale air. I pull the pillows from the bed and stack them beneath the window, but they are encased in cheap chintz and slippery as catgut. I disembowel them and this time their bobbled innards Velcro together and stay put. I take out the Parker-Hale, assemble it and take aim.

It is only twelve minutes past two. I have seventeen more minutes before The Target will appear, eighteen before he will be dead, twenty before I will be on my way back home. Twenty-six before the police will be at the scene, scratching and shaking their heads. I check the door is locked and chained, and sweep the room once more with the Glock. Its muzzle stares through the shower curtains, into the cupboards, round the doors. There's a lonely bible in the drawer by the bed, UHT milk on a plastic tray by the kettle. No-one is waiting in the wardrobe for me with garrotting wire. I am satisfied. It's a tiny room; there aren't many places to hide.

Two sixteen. I swap the under-stuffed pillows for a comely cushion from the frayed and faded sofa. The cushion is solid to kneel on and I do, and this feels more comfortable than the pillows. I wait.

The room is above a wide road cruised by expensive cars and rust-riddled death-traps in equal measure. The road divides two areas of starkly contrasting wealth, each notorious in its own right. On this side of the street are, mostly, cheap hotels and cheaper shops above which tenants are crammed into spaces barely fit for habitation.

On the other side are cafés, boutiques, department stores, a mini-Ritz, a cheaper Harrods. No corner shops or newsagents, no greengrocers. Only elitist nightclubs and terribly upmarket shops. A fake sun warms the sunny side of this street.

In the middle of the road, dividing the flows of traffic, is a narrow stretch of grass surrounded by black railings, mosaic-ed with purple and white pansies. The word etched in a slab of stone is *Welcome*. Welcome to our little Hell.

The hotel is on Mason Street, not Mason Road. The incongruousness grates. I cannot put my finger on it, but this place feels wrong to me. Perhaps it is not the place, but the situation. I have never felt this uneasy on a mission before. THEY would not have done it on purpose, I'm sure, but the timings of The Fax yesterday and The Phone Call the day before have left a bitter, metallic taste in my mouth. My clocks are not wrong; I am meticulous about that.

Two twenty. There are two .308 bullets in the chamber of the Parker-Hale. I concentrate on the job at hand and close one eye and press the other to the telescopic sight. The hotel opposite is a tall, broad, Edwardian affair, doubtless with all the mod-cons the Edwardians had to do without. The porter, smart in crimson, stands beside a red carpet. He holds the door open and smiles politely as the money walks past.

Two twenty two. Jeremiah did a great job getting us in, with his easy smile and casual demeanour, and the desk clerk (no porter for this flea-pit) was too busy counting his notes and envying his confidence to wonder what was in the large black case I held.

Something in the corner of my eye makes me pull back from the scope in consternation. The concierge has appeared outside the hotel opposite and is muttering something to the porter, but that is not what concerns me.

What concerns me, almost frightens me, is the sun, glinting on the curve of the concierge's gold buttons. Until now it has been hidden behind buildings to my right, but it has begun to move round and suddenly its edge is needling light down into my scope, into my eyes. Those warm, bright rays send fear coursing through my blood.

Why didn't THEY check the sun's position when they assigned me this Mission, this time, this room? It is THEIR job, not mine, to take care of such details.

I put a hand to my chest and feel the quickened beating of my heart. THEY are usually so careful, so precise.

THEY never make mistakes…but THEY've made one now. I must wait another…four minutes before I take The Shot. How far will the sun have moved in four minutes? Will it shine into my eyes and spoil my aim? Will it compromise The Mission? Will it glint on my scope and give me away?

Two twenty six. It is inching round the building, bit by bit. Almost half is revealed now. The concierge has come and gone but the porter is enjoying the warmth on his face. What should I do? I wipe the sweat from my forehead with the back of my hand and take deep breaths to ease the shuddering of my frame. Nothing like this has ever happened before, not in sixty-four Missions. Not to any of us.

Two twenty seven. I am not used to distractions, but one leads to another and suddenly I am thinking about the girl downstairs. The way she looked when she came to my door last night, her short dark hair pinned back carelessly, as if she didn't own a mirror. Her small lips red as if she'd been biting them…concentrate! What's wrong with you? Never mind the way she smelled…

Two twenty eight. She had a white t-shirt on, a kid's t-shirt, too tight at the arms. Showed an inch of navel. 'H²0, the way to go' in blue letters across her breasts…

Two twenty nine. The Target's stepping out of the hotel, a smug grin on his face. Navy slacks, blue shoes, pinstripe white shirt. Suit jacket over one arm, because it's hot in the sun. Because he's been fucking like a rabbit up in room 42. Because his toupee's on a little cock-eyed.

Jeremiah's here now, slowly taking over the job I set up for him to do. I am pushed aside, along with all my little fears. It is *his* hand on the rifle, *his* finger on the trigger, *his* eye to the scope. It is *he* who traces The Target down the steps towards his chauffeur-driven corporate-executive Mercedes stretch. I have set it up, but it is *he* who caresses the trigger. *Jeremiah*, just once, just once…

But, somehow, it is me who feels The Shot.

~

I didn't go home straight away. I moved casually, unseen, between the screaming onlookers and slipped quietly out of Mason Street. I scuffed the sidewalk with my weary feet and somehow found my way into the park, sitting on the bench that Jeanie died for and staring at the floating surface of the pond.

I don't remember any children playing in the park. I don't remember the ducks. I only remember concealing the Parker-Hale in an alley and ensuring no-one saw me do it. I do the same each time, so that in the confusion following The Shot I am not caught carrying what may be a trumpet, or might be a rifle. I will go back for it later.

The sun is warm on my skin, but I don't feel it. Jeremiah chats away animatedly about himself, but I don't want to hear. His white teeth, his smooth skin, his soft dark hair and soft dark eyes. Eyes like Demerara sugar and molasses. Mine feel like vinegar. I am sour all through.

The afternoon fades into evening and still I sit, too numb to move. I can't help thinking about the three children whose father I…whose father Jeremiah just killed. Something about the whole thing strikes a bitter note with me – a note that has not been struck before, in any of the Missions.

I don't want to go back home and find the last paperwork for Mission 65 hanging from the fax machine. I don't want to acknowledge that this Mission almost didn't go to plan – that a subtle shift in my normality, starting with THEIR timings being out and culminating in an error that could have compromised me, has left me disturbed by the feeling that *something isn't right.* Is it HER suddenly presence in my life that has so drastically changed everything? Is it that Jeremiah, for all his calm composure and apparent virtue, seems as ill-suited to me as a too-small pair of gloves?

Is it that I can still feel his sickly, persistent presence when he should already have taken his leave?

I want to talk to the girl downstairs again, or rather to listen. When I think about her I feel calm inside, as if Jeremiah is nothing in her world. I wonder what *I* am in her world. The guy upstairs who shot a hole through her ceiling with a bottle of Jacob's Creek Chardonnay.

The sunset spills lilac dyes into the pond and stains the ducks and swans a cloudy pink. Oblivious, they mill and quack and preen. I realise it is growing late. My skin is dotted with geese. I should go back.

As I rise to leave, I finally notice how empty the park is – or has become. There is no-one walking the path around the pond, no-one sitting on the other benches or throwing croutons of bread to the overfed pigeons. The trees rustle and whisper and fall still. The shadows shrink and disappear.

My shoes tap and click, yet the cars make no sound. Jeremiah makes no sound. I feel quite alone.

Yet I am not alone, I realise, as two men emerge behind me and begin to follow me through the park. Their sneakers are silent, their breathing muffled. I swallow and pick up my pace. They match it. My hand reaches for the Glock. They rush forward.

The barrel snags on exiting the holster; I cannot free my gun in time.

They bear me to the ground.

~

I'm choking, gagging, drowning. The water tastes like blood. It's in my mouth, my throat, my nose and ears and eyes. I'm breathing nails and spitting iron. Someone is tap-dancing against the fragile paper of my skull. Their shoes are soled with broken glass.

I don't know why, but I didn't die that night. I don't know how, but I staggered across the road and stumbled up the stairs of my apartment block. The stairs were slick with someone's blood. What had happened here?

Nothing, Jeremiah tells me. *It's your blood, numbskull.*

I wish my skull was numb, because they smacked it with a crowbar. I don't know who they were, but they beat me half to death.

Ouch. Ouch. Ouch. The stairs are jagged. They rise to meet me, oh so softly, then speed up and hit me in the face. When I stagger to my feet again they laugh, and wobble with their jollity.

I am exhausted. I cannot climb another step. I cannot scale this mountain. Someone has replaced my oxygen with tear gas. My eyes are streaming, I am wheezing, the breath is bubbling in my chest. Everything hurts, *oh God, it hurts.*

I think this is my door. It looks the same. My hands are oily and the key slips to the floor.

I reach to pick it up and the floor hits me in the face again. The door falls on my head.

"What the hell…" the door says, then moves aside as I look up to find the girl downstairs standing in the doorway of my flat. Of course, it isn't my flat, it's hers. She's wearing shorts and a shirt two X's too L. She stares down at me, eyes wide with shock.

"Oh my God…" she gasps, hand fluttering to her mouth like the wing of a frightened moth. She hovers for a moment, then is gone, drawn to some other flame.

Stage??? Gone to Heaven

I think I spoke to God to last night. I think He decided He had some higher purpose for me than to die a miserable and lonely death on the floor outside the girl downstairs' apartment. I seem to remember that he lifted me up and out of my agony, and deposited me neatly on a cloud, where I lay in a state of quite pleasant euphoria for what may, or may not, have been many aeons. I waited and waited and waited for Him, and eventually He came.

His face was hidden. All I saw was a white sheet. A really big, Persil-white, freshly-ironed sheet. It could have been His robes, if God wears robes. He covered me with this white sheet and sat down on the cloud beside me, making the whole thing tilt furiously until I felt quite sick.

And when He spoke, the strangest words came from His mouth, and in the strangest voice, which was not at all as I had imagined God's voice to be, if He has one at all.

"You stupid bastard," He said softly, in a woman's voice. A rather nice woman's voice, actually. "You stupid, bloody, bloodied-up bastard."

God really *is* a woman! I thought, deliriously. Blimey, there's a thing.

"There's blood all over my bloody sofa, you stupid bastard," God said, still softly, but rather lacking the compassion I had imagined He/She would show one of His/Her children.

"I'll phone for an ambulance," He/She went on, stroking my face with a hand that was both freezing cold and soaking wet, as if God was in fact some kind of omnipotent arctic seal. "You really need to get to hospital..."

Alarm at the Almighty's divine words punched through my fog, caused me to breach the boundaries of Heaven and Earth as I reached out to grab the sopping hand.

I think it must have been about that point when I realised that God felt very human, and that His wrist was quite small and fragile enough to be a woman's wrist, and that He was in fact holding a cold soggy sponge now pinkish with blood, and that I was lying on a sofa, covered with a sheet, and that God was, in actuality, the girl downstairs, who looked more like Mary Magdalene having caught Jesus quietly sneaking back the keys to the donkey-cart after a night out on the town. But, and it could have been my jangled brain playing tricks on me, I did think that I detected a small amount of concern in Her dark brown eyes.

She tries to pull away, extracts from me a whimper of pain, and attempts to more gently extricate herself from my grasp.

I shake my head feebly, desperately, as she reaches for the phone.

Please, I beg her, too weak to do more than whisper and cling monkey-like to her slender wrist. *Don't phone for an ambulance. I'll be alright. Please don't call anyone.*

Looking up at her, I felt like I was watching a widescreen film on an old and incompatible TV. The top and bottom edges were black and slightly blurred, and the field of vision in the middle was a narrow band that grew narrower as the bruised borders closed in. My widescreen siren stared back at me with clouded eyes, neat brows stitched together in confusion at my strange request, anger at my having bloodied-up her sofa, and a reluctant realisation that she may just care enough to heed my plea.

I think she finally acquiesced, for she left the phone to its own devices and went to fetch something for me. I don't remember what it was; I was too busy fainting to take much care.

~

Dawn is a painful time. There is no beauty in the sunrise, whose vicious light punishes me for having woken it with my feeble coughing. The birds squawk and screech and chatter vindictively in both my ears. The semi-peace of half-sleep is shattered and ground down to sand.

But I am more coherent than I was last night. I have given Death the slip again, and one glance at the opposing sofa tells me how. The girl downstairs (can I call her that, now that I am on her floor?) is curled up and asleep, exhausted from her vigil through the night.

She has nursed me back to health (Why? What has she to gain?) but now a rabid fear bites my heart. What will happen to her because of me? She will certainly ask questions, and what do I tell her? What do I tell THEM?

Sitting makes me giddy and nauseous but I do it anyway. I do it *in spite*. Both hands grip the sofa-seat white-knuckled as the walls sashay. There are no solids in this world, only liquids. The boundaries of the room are water, the ceiling is an ocean and I am at its bed, and the pressure is so great I feel my ears begin to bleed.

Then I see The Hole, the hole a .45 calibre Jacob's Creek Chardonnay cork made in the floor, and I catch a glimpse of my *own* ceiling. I am amazed! Amazed both at my own stupidity and at the fact that I can see *my* ceiling from the floor below!

The trek to the bathroom could be up a mountain. Each step is rocky, the air tastes thin, and my feet are planted without coordination as if narrowly missing boulders. I cannot help but think of Jeremiah, whose feet land on track as if drawn by magnets. I try to take strength from Max, the memory of his sureness and agility, but only find loneliness and uncertainty where his confidence used to be.

The bathroom is clean but untidy. I prepare to recoil with Jeremiah's fear of mess, but feel nothing. Just a shrugging, *who-cares* feeling. It doesn't matter.

The room smells different to my own. Nice. Not that my own does not smell nice. But this room...this smells sweet, like a woman. Soap and vanilla musk and potpourri.

The carpet is soft and for the first time I realise I am barefoot, wearing nothing but my boxer shorts beneath the white sheet I shrugged off and left across the sofa.

The room is small but not narrow, made more spacious and bright by the wide mirror on one wall. I squint and wince simultaneously as I confront the poor bastard it reflects.

He looks like an overripe banana; slightly crooked and covered in bruises. He has two black eyes, a broken-looking nose, a break in the skin below one eye where a sharp-ish cheekbone grazed some passing knuckles. A crowbar-shaped lump across the forehead and right temple is a source of intense pain, having swollen to Great-Wall-of-China-proportions. The lip is split and bloated like an overdose of collagen.

The body is little better off. Left shoulder hideously dislocated, though strangely numb (except when I move, or breath, or sigh, flinch, swallow, blink, etc) and the ribs are black and blue and pretty shades of purple that stretch across the stomach and dapple the chest. Not a broad chest, but not narrow either. The body is not so different from my own.

I pad to the sink and turn on the taps. My hands are shaking. Water rises and the sound is almost delicious. I splash my face, find a small towel, dampen it and wipe away the blood that has seeped since she fell asleep.

The cut lip will heal, the bruises will fade, my vision will return to its normal parameters in a few days once the swelling has gone down. The ribs are cracked and sore, but none broken. I know the pain of broken ribs and it is otherworldly.

My memory of last night is distorted, a drunken switching on and off of remembrance. The two men were but shadows in the failing light, but there are elements of their attack that remain clear and my sleep-refreshed brain makes notes:

- The park was empty
- Both men wore trainers, indicating a premeditated attack (or possibly joggers)
- Neither man was deterred when I went for the Glock - either they were expecting me to be armed, or were determined enough to disregard thoughts of their own safety when they realised I had a gun
- If they had meant to kill me, they would have done so. No weapons, save the crowbar, were used; no blades, no guns. This was meant to look unprofessional…

I stopped myself short. *Look* unprofessional? Where had I got the idea that this was a *professional* attack?

Bile rose in my throat as I considered the potential implications of such a chain of thought. Could this be THEIR work, I wondered, then smacked my dislocated shoulder back into its socket against the wall before Jeremiah or anyone else could voice protest.

Off in the distance, a wolf howled. Long, loud, heartfelt, and sorrowful. A wounded wolf, one with its legs caught in the bitter jaws of a hunter's trap; and the hunter only a few dozen metres away, footsteps muffled by the snow.

I had about half a second to think how strange it was that I could hear a wolf, then I staggered to the toilet and vomited, violently and repeatedly, because each retch wrenched my ribs and the pain only triggered further sickness.

Footsteps, muffled by the carpet. I didn't know she was behind me until I felt her hand on my back. Sleep-warm skin. She ran it, reassuringly, up and down my spine, rubbing between my shoulders and the back of my neck until I sank back against her, whole body shaking, feeling her warmth permeate my through-and-through chill. She wrapped both arms around me and started to rock me, as if I was a child.

As far back as I can recall, I have removed myself deliberately from human contact. Handshakes, hugs, standing close on the subway or the bus or in the elevator. I remove myself from these contacts by avoiding the situations that incur them. I walk, always in the road and not on the pavement. I climb the stairs, never take the lift.

I do not make friends, or meet others in the flesh. I do not go to my neighbours for help, because I have never needed help before now.

But the soft, warm skin, the two X's too L t-shirt, the smell of soap and vanilla, the dark silk of her hair, the touch of her hands…these I can no longer avoid, because, right now, I need them. I need to be reassured, I need to be comforted.

I need not to be alone.

But alone is safe. Together…together is danger multiplied by two, and I'm afraid now that I may bring danger to this woman, this angel, with whom I feel I am beginning to fall in love.

The Death of a Friend

I dragged my sorry self up the single flight of stairs that separated my world from hers and shut the door, very quietly.

Nothing had been disturbed. I knew before Jeremiah's orderly arrangements even met my eye that no-one had been up here, because I would have seen them through the hole in the floor.

The light on the fax machine was flashing angrily. The paper was out.

I refilled it and stepped back, finger hesitating over the button. What was I afraid of? What did I think I would read on that mocking white tongue? I looked for Max but he was gone, silently refusing me his courage. I hit GO and went to the kitchen.

Like the light at the end of the tunnel, I spied my kettle. Aah, precious warmth, precious life. I fondly stroked its plastic shell and filled it to the 4-cup mark. I would make, and drink, that many cups before I returned to read The Fax.

Almost a minute passed before I registered the sound of silence. It blocked up my every other sense, filling the kitchen with emptiness that the birdie-whir starting up in the next room could not drown out.

Horror filtered into me. No steam! No boil!

My nightmare has come true – the kettle doesn't work.

~

It's not just a fuse, it is the *whole kettle.*

I grope blindly in the cupboards for a spare, reining in my panic, but know deep down there is none to be had. Perhaps a saucepan will do; I can boil the teabag on the hob.

More groping results in stubbed fingers, breathlessness from sore ribs that should be resting, and a pan. The water takes an eternity to boil. I throw in *six* teabags *(stirred eighteen times anti-clockwise)* and *twelve* spoons of sugar, to compensate for shock of finding the kettle dead. Milk is sloshed in by unsteady hand and subsequently burnt onto pan and hob.

At last – tea. Three large mugs of piping hot, stewed tea. Tea leaves float about within, because one of the teabags has taken it upon itself to burst. The scum occupying the top layer is the result of greasy metal and slightly rancid milk. I don't care. Jeremiah, who seems to have abandoned me to suffer alone, isn't around to have a fit over my lapse in hygiene, and Max, for all his let's-throw-caution-to-the-wind attitude, could never stomach the smell of sour milk, and for once I am glad he is gone.

My body is sore, the throbbing pain of my stubbed fingers far outweighed by the ache of an all-over coat of bruises.

I drink to forget the pain, or rather to replace it with new, for the tea is still boiling a little in the cup, and sears the tender flesh of my mouth.

Still, it lends a warm, comforting lining to my stomach and I feel easier than I have since the Mission.

What a bizarre drink, I think; whoever would have thought that stewed leaves and sour milk could be so euphoric?

As I drain the third cup and spit out fragments of leaf that have stuck to teeth and lips, I remember with a heavy heart the fax machine, whose incessant song has silenced, but whose grim threat remains.

I pop my head around the kitchen door, groaning as bruises stretch over aching muscles.

The Fax is a long one.

About six pages long.

Long enough to be intimidating.

Long, long, long.

Ah, stop farting around. Go and get the bloody thing.

So I do, and it is not what I have been dreading. Not, 'Why are you associating with the girl downstairs?' – it is merely the final paperwork regarding Mission 65. Paperwork I must read, verify, and destroy. Like the other sixty-four sets of paperwork I have read, verified and destroyed in my career.

Like the other sixty-four sets of paperwork I have not tucked away in The Mission Files.

If THEY knew about The Files, I would not live to see the sunrise.

The last page of The Fax is a neatly printed enquiry after my health:

Hi there,

How are you feeling?

Hope everything is okay. I haven't heard from you in a while.

I am fine, as is the cat.

I was sorry to hear your uncle had died. I hope you weren't close.

If you need to talk, you know where I am.

P.S. Thank you for the lovely weekend.

Susan

The follow-ups are always like that. Encrypted, *just* in case they fall into the wrong hands. *Just* in case your meddling next-door neighbour barges in, looking for some sugar, and stumbles across a neatly-printed message with the details of your last assassination.

The follow-ups are always written in code. It's never easy to decipher, because two messages are never alike in style. But in my profession, you have to learn to read between the lines.

~

I dozed for most of the afternoon, drifting in and out of sleep, or perhaps consciousness, and woke when it was dark to repeated and urgent banging at my door. I was propped up against the sofa, as opposed to on it; probably afraid I'd fall off.

I rose, giddily, staggered a few steps, and fell over. Legs too weak. Can't…stand. Want to…sleep. Big…baby. Hey…watch who…you're calling…a baby.

I crawled the rest of the way, trying frantically to think where I'd stowed the Glock. Had I dropped it in the park? Or thrown it in the alleyway with the Parker-Hale? (Note to self: must rescue Parker-Hale before bin-men find it. Also, must buy new kettle.)

I reach the door and try to look under, but the motion of tilting my head makes my stomach swoop and I stop. I stand, hauling myself up by the handle, scuffing against the wall, banging into the door in my dizziness. I wish I had my Glock on me, then realise that I have just made plenty enough noise to announce my presence, and that if my visitor was an assassin, or the two bad men returning to kick me around some more, they would have bashed the door down already. I pull it open.

Her face is flushed, her eyes fever-bright, her hand raised in a fist to pound again. She is caught off-guard as I open the door, and narrowly avoids punching me in the face.

"Stupid bastard!" she starts; a yell at first, then her protests drop to angry whispers as the decibel-level registers on my face. Concern creases her smooth lines, then anger, then a confusion of the two. "I've been knocking for hours! I thought you were dead."

I invite her in. She hesitates, but only for a moment. I shut the door behind her, and deliberate, for the first time, about whether or not to lock it. I *always* lock the door.

"You have a lovely view," she muses, standing at the window, looking at the park. She has the same view from her window as I have from mine.

"Oh, I know," she says airily. "But you're higher up than me. It seems different, somehow. Almost…omnipotent."

I stand beside her, staring out at the night-dark park. The trees and grass are blue, the pond almost black. The swans are asleep on the bank, long necks curled around and heads tucked away beneath their wings, blind to the darkness.

Before I know it, I am leaning on her. She doesn't seem to mind, standing like a rock as she takes my weight. She is slim, but powerful. Her arms were strong as they supported me last night, and strong as they encircled me, and strong as they comforted me. She lives alone, works alone, eats alone. I intruded on her solitude last night. She doesn't seem to mind it, now.

This is the first time she has been inside my flat, and suddenly my home seems more…3D.

"Do you want something to drink?" she asks. "Do you mind if I make some tea?"

I tell her, voice thick with choked emotion, that the kettle is dead.

"What?" she exclaims, and recoils from me in a manner of horror, as if I had just told her who I really was. "Dead? What do you mean? How? How can it be dead?"

This registers some surprise in me. Does she really feel the same way I do about the kettle? I nod my head sadly and she pulls away, swinging through the door and leaving me alone. I look after her, sorrowfully, mournfully – mourning her leaving, mourning the kettle. Perhaps I should bury it. It has died and she has left me.

Perhaps she left me because the idea of being without a kettle was abhorrent to her. It certainly would be to me, if only I could stop thinking how much my face hurts.

Now she is back, pounding on the door again. My movements are painfully keen as I walk to it, open it, and find her standing in the hallway, bright against the bland decay of the walls.

Holding a kettle in her hands.

What an angel.

~

We drank tea from big mugs, sat side-by-side on the sofa which she turned to face the window. We can only see the sky, but it is blind-blue and cloudless and studded with flickering points of light.

She is mostly silent, hands cupped around the warmth. I slurp, wincing as the steam burns my sore face, and relish the sensation as the tea slides down and settles in a muddy ocean in my stomach.

I glance sideways at her face from time to time, trying not to let her see me do it.

She has a strange profile, utterly different from mine. Small nose, long lashes, small ripe lips. Little apples for cheeks. Long, slim neck. Her hair is pinned up – not neatly, but the mess is endearing. It is very short like this, gives her elfin features.

I can't help myself, but my hand begins to stray. It strays across the sofa back, adolescent in its clumsiness. It wanders upwards, touches the silky dark strands of her hair. Before it knows its own mind, it is working the first clips free.

She tips her head back a little, pressing it against my hand, and looks at me.

I flinch, expecting rejection. Expecting to find my arm slapped away, or hot tea thrown in my face. Or to see her simply rise and walk out of my life.

But she does none of these things. She nuzzles her cheek against my rough palm and closes her eyes, cat-like, and lets me pull out the rest of the clips.

Her hair falls down, short and messy and soft against my fingers. I lean in close, just because I have the sudden urge to bury my face in her soft hair and smell the soap and vanilla musk.

Just because I might breathe her in, and swallow her up inside of me.

Just because I need to feel something other than pain.

And she turns her face a little further as I do it, catching my cheek with her lips. Her breath is warm and smells of tea and sugar and something else as sweet. Ever, ever so gently, mindful of my bruises, she raises a tea-warmed hand and caresses my scarred face. Ever, ever so gently, she pulls me in towards her and brushes her lips against mine.

The feeling is electricity, cold shivers, hot flushes, a long cold drink on a hot summer's day. Sneezing five times in a row. Tea and toast in winter. Someone breathing on the back of your neck. Someone walking over your grave. A feather tickling the tips of your fingers, the soles of your feet. Waves rushing up the sand and swallowing your ankles. A cool breeze through the acacia trees as the sun burns your skin. Ice cream, brain-freeze, sensitive teeth. Doing something naughty for the first time. Getting caught. Getting away with it.

But nothing can describe the feeling of her tongue, tiny and soft, warm and gentle, parting my lips, running its wet body around my tongue and deep into my mouth until I am overwhelmed with the urge to bite it off or swallow it whole. The taste is like eating sugar from a spoon, crunching each grain, feeling alive and sick, and longing for more.

She is the nectar of the sweetest, brightest flower, and I am the bee, drawn to her, trapped by her. Killed by her. I am the honey-maker. I am the artist. I can fly, but I decide not to test the theory, not just yet.

No Pleasure without the Pain

I wake in the morning to find she is gone. My bed is an ocean, big and deep. I am alone, I cannot find shore. I cannot swim. I cannot sleep.

The sheets are rumpled, her pillow dented. I sink my face into it and smell her there, trace the outline of her body with my finger, close my eyes and remember the velvet of her skin, the silk of her hair, the softness of her.

I open my eyes and the room is bright with sunshine, warm with light. I rise and barely notice the pain. My floor is carpeted with cloud.

The apartment is bright and warm and white and cool. There is space I never knew I had. The painting on the wall is a masterpiece, an exquisite work of art. I want to dance to the music in my head.

I love the world
I love my life
I've fallen in love with a beautiful girl
And I want to make her my wife

I float into the kitchen and feel myself smile – she has made the ultimate sacrifice and left me her kettle. I fondle it into life and make the best-tasting tea ever.

Couple of teabags, some sugar. Bit of milk that isn't off.

I waltz back out to the living room, to the sofa we sat on, to the window we looked through and saw a world outside bathed in darkness, when our world in here, together, was cosy and warm and alight. I caress the sofa, imagine that her hair is still splayed across the cushion.

There is a white piece of paper on the table, I see. Maybe she has written me a love letter. I dance across and pick it up.

The blood freezes and stands still in my veins, my heart stops its beats. The tea turns to ash in my mouth.

Mission 66 is printed in bold at the top of The Fax, hemmed with a date and a time.

And below, in grainy black and white, is a picture of the girl downstairs.

66: Stage One – The Phone Call

The Call came this afternoon at precisely thirty-seven minutes and eighteen seconds past four. It was still the wrong time, but at least it was the same wrong time as before; I suppose there is some reassurance in that.

I answered The Call, calmly, as I methodically worked over the Parker-Hale. I rescued it earlier from the alley and it was little the worse for wear, though I would clean it anyway. A kamikaze mouse had nibbled a hole in the case and made a starter home in the trigger-guard with shreds of cotton wool.

I was sure to disassemble the rifle first, this time, and divest it of its corks.

The Voice was cool, smooth and oily. It relayed to me information regarding The Target – information I already knew.

- Gender: Female
- Height: 5'6"
- Build: Small, slight
- Hair: Dark
- Eyes: Dark
- Occupation: Switchboard operator (I didn't know this)

Something is seriously wrong. I stand by the phone, heart thumping, hand hovering.

I must call THEM back. I must ask THEM why she is The Target. I must *know*.

But I cannot – I *never* contact THEM, THEY always contact me. Us. Mickey, Ned, Gerald, Jack, Robert, Harry, Jeremiah, Max. We have always been at THEIR whim, THEIR disposal. When THEY have finished with us, we disappear. I do not exist. I have never existed.

But she has made me be. She and her silky dark hair, her velvety skin, her rosebud lips and wide, dark eyes. She, with her gentle hands and violent kisses. *She* has made me *be*.

I will not do this. Not without knowing why. How can *she* be The Target?

I sit cross-legged on the floor, fingers steepled. The Parker-Hale rests across my thighs.

I close my eyes and think about the two men in the park two days ago, whose fists and feet like leeches bled me almost dry. I think about the whites of their trainers, the whites of their eyes. I wonder how THEY knew I would be there…

The truth is a colourless, odourless drug. It seeps into my body and is in my brain before I even realise I have thought of it. It is so excruciatingly simple.

THEY want rid of me. THEY set up Mission 65; THEY set it up to fail – no, not to fail, but to fail ME. THEY had two men try to kill me…no, not kill. If THEY had wanted me dead, I would be. To hurt me, to force me…to force me into her arms. But why? Because anyone who gets too close, anyone who tries to know me, anyone who knows anything about me…must be eliminated.

It is too dangerous for me to have any connections. THEY sent me to her, and now THEY ask me to kill her.

Is this a test? Are THEY testing my loyalty and commitment to THEM?

Or am I being betrayed.

66: Stage Two – The Target

I went shopping today. I was stared at collectively by mothers pushing monkeys in prams, partners kissing and holding hands, shopkeepers keeping shop as I tried not to look at my warped reflection in their windows.

I am Ned today. I am used to being stared at.

I am Robert today. I am used to being ignored.

I am Gerald today. I am better than all of them.

I am Jack today. I can't see them for the cloud of smoke.

I am Eric today. I would like to cut them all down.

I am Harry today. I think the whole world needs to get a fucking life.

I am Jeremiah today. I walk without watching where I place my feet.

I am Max today. I do not care that people stare. I am a predator. I wear the scars of battle proudly.

The swelling has gone down, but my face is still dark with bruises. I wince as I walk, as bruises mash together and cracked ribs jar. In a supermarket I sneer at the customers who stare as if they have no eyelids. For the first time I am conspicuous, without the shelter of another man's identity. For the first time I am naked in front of all their eyes.

My hair is short, dark, soft – like hers. My eyes are almost blue, but slightly grey. My teeth are white and straight but for one slightly crooked canine. I have a scar above my left eyebrow, another on my jaw.

Geneva gave my nose a little break, just on the bridge, and it is visible once again beneath the more recent trauma.

When I looked into the mirror as I brushed my teeth, I felt as if I'd come across an old friend.

Run over an old friend, more like, I mused, and bought a tin of beans. I picked up teabags and even some coffee. I *never* drink coffee. At least, I never have before.

I choose every item that is strange to me; tinned apricots, blueberry jam, bananas, sandwich spread, pickled olives, mushroom pate, dried spaghetti, meringue, frankfurters, brioche, raspberry trifle, sirloin steak, chocolate milk, pasta sauce.

I stop at an art supply shop and buy an easel, paints and brushes – I don't know why, I do not paint, and so it makes no sense that I should buy these things now, but perhaps it is because I feel like I could paint a masterpiece.

Brasso, pipe cleaners, WD40, lighter fluid and matches are procured from a hardware store.

White mice and liquorice laces are carried squeaking from the sweet shop.

I stop at a café and stare at the tuna sandwiches and iced lattes. I hate tuna. I want a steak slice, dripping with fat and piping hot. I want to lick greasy fingers Jeremiah would rather cut off. I feel like an animal, like Max. I buy an ice cream and let it melt down the cone and across my fingers as I nibble the six flakes I have stuck into the creamy top. I am *not* Max.

I have my Glock back. I had left it downstairs, in her flat. It had slid under the sofa when I stumbled through her door and fell on my face. She had found it, cleaned it, left it on my table, next to The Fax with her picture on it.

I haven't seen her since, but I hear her switch on the TV and clatter some pans, and I smell the food she cooks for herself. I hear her talking to the stray cat she feeds and loves. It strayed up to my floor once and stalked across my bed as I slept. It made me wake with a jump and I yelled, and must have scared it, because it meowed loudly and buried all four sets of claws into my arm.

The Glock is tucked snugly under my left arm in its holster, feeling more than comfortable there.

I plan on cooking dinner tonight, for me and the girl downstairs. Nothing fancy, just pasta in sauce and some wine, with a trifle for dessert. I tingle with the anticipation of seeing her again, but am fearful of her reaction to the Glock and The Fax. Will she demand to know why I have a gun, or why her face is on the message headed **Mission 66**? Maybe she'll wait until I'm cooking, then stab me in the back with a fork.

My mind is full of questions today, which is nice. Nice to think about questions when you're being stared at like some kind of freak.

I think of what I will do about the girl downstairs, about whether I will carry out The Mission. I only know half of the answer, but the rest will come.

I think about THEM and what THEY are up to, because I'm sure there's something amiss. It began with the errors of Mission 65; the second Call coming seven seconds early (I know now that this was a deliberate mistake), the sun in my eyes as I took aim at The Target, and Mission 66 began with a Fax. The Missions *always* begin with a Call.

I have made up my mind. I *must* contact THEM. It breaks all the rules, but I have broken so many already. I keep The Files when I should have destroyed them. I have initiated relations with an outsider. I am questioning THEM.

When I return home, I see the old man sitting at his window, staring hatefully at the park. When I walk by, he looks hatefully at me.

I don't go to my floor straight away – I go to hers. I knock and there is no reply, just the sound of a hairdryer and the TV chattering away. I knock again, louder, and thump the door with my un-shot foot, just for good measure. She switches off the hairdryer and moments later appears in place of the door.

Mmm, she is in a towel.

I ask her to come to mine for dinner, telling her I'll cook pasta. She smiles sweetly, shakes her head, and utters words that break my heart.

"Actually, I have a date."

Am lost for words. *A date?* With someone else? But, I thought…

"Sorry. Hey, I'll see you around, okay?" And she shuts the door.

I slope upstairs with my shopping and feel empty inside. She has stabbed me in the back with the fork and then scooped me hollow with her trifle spoon.

My thoughts are coagulated and messy, filled with memories of our passion. She made me feel *alive* – how can she then kill me again?

I am heartless and numb as I slam the door behind me.

Just because it can, because it *takes pleasure* in doing so, the handle of my shopping bag breaks.

It is the bag containing all the jars of pasta sauce and bottles of wine. They land on my foot – my *shot* foot. The pain is like a flare in the darkness of my grief, and suddenly I am Max all over again. I curse, shout, hop on one foot and bang my head on a passing shelf. Foul swear words ooze from my mouth, which only this morning was birthing poetry and music.

There is nothing but anger inside me now, and before I know what I'm doing I have freed the Glock from its holster and am aiming it at the most eye-catching object in the room.

The painting. It becomes the target of my fury and receives six bullets for its ugliness. Each shot fires shock through my hands, up my arms, into my aching shoulders, all through my bruised body, resounding in my throbbing head until I can taste the metal in my mouth.

I have not tasted anything so exquisite since she kissed me.

I drop the Glock and find the Parker-Hale, removing it from its case and lovingly caressing the polished barrel, the smoothed butt...the solid trigger. Its resistance makes me press harder, harder, slowly harder, until sweat breaks out on my brow and my hands shake. Power surges in my blood. I *want* to pull the trigger. I *want* to kill somebody.

I go to the window and take aim at the park. A child, playing on a swing. Another kicking a ball through a flowerbed. A little girl throwing bits of bread at the ducks, then running away giggling, then running back to throw more.

One...little...squeeze. It would be so easy. It would erase all my pain.

But I am not angry at that little girl. I am angry at another girl, a girl who lives downstairs. A girl whose ceiling I shot through. A girl who has betrayed me. *That* is who my anger is for. *That* is who I will pull the trigger for.

Mission 66 is on.

66: Stage Three – Becoming Max…again

I sit alone in the darkness, legs crossed, hands clasped coolly, staring ahead through my eyelids. I am entirely still. I do not even breathe. I am a lion, I am stalking my prey through the long grass of the African plain. Stealth is the key. Stealth, patience, stamina, strength, stillness.

Max nurses his gun – not the Glock of my preference, but a Colt KingCobra .357 magnum. Leaning against the chair, its cold muzzle on his naked forearm, is the Russian Dragunov I so despise. Max loves this rifle. It is an animal, a brute of a weapon. It has no finesse, no neatness to it. It tears holes in flesh. It is Max through and through.

It is not my choice that Max is here. He arrived unannounced and barged his way in, not taking no as an answer, refusing to leave me alone. He is persistent, threatening, frightening. Even I am not safe with Max around.

Max is what fuels my hatred now. There are many parts of me that cannot think of her as an enemy, a Target to be killed. In my heart, though I am hurt, I cannot hate her. She has given me so much.

She has made me remember who I am…who I was, before Max turned up.

Max will hear none of it. He is determined that she has caused us the most grievous pain and suffering, and that she should be made to pay for it.

I fought him, at first. I told him, *I don't want to hurt her*. But Max does. Max wants her dead. His pride has been insulted – no-one who insults Max's pride *ever* escapes unscathed.

She has not returned yet from her *date*. Max spits the word. He talks to me, in a voice so soft it demands attention, as a teacher would a naughty child, telling me what a fool I have been for allowing myself to be used by this viperess. He calls her The Medusa. His tone is hateful and tender; he loves me as a brother, loathes me for my weakness. He despises me, for I am not like him, yet I am as good as blood kin, and he cannot turn his back on me. He will protect me from The Medusa and from myself...but if I humiliate him again, he will tear me apart.

~

I'm hungry. Max has sat still for hours, and I am confined to a world where nothing remains of me but my hunger. I am encaged by Max's anger, frightened by his hatred, whipped by his scorn. He cares nothing for my feelings any more, only his own wounded pride. He has even forgotten about THEM and refuses to admit THEIR betrayal as I shout it at him. He will not rise to read The Fax that has arrived, whilst I yearn to know what is printed there. It is an unannounced document. THEY have never sent one at this hour before.

My hunger is growing, a bubbling pit into which my mind is falling fast. I am so tired I can scarcely keep open my eyes, but Max stabs me into wakefulness each time I start to drift. He is the centre of a universe of concentration, the sun around which all else must orbit. His magnetism is beginning to drag everything else into the searing heat and I am burning, slowly burning.

But, no matter the strength of Max's commitment to staring blankly into space, my curiosity eventually gets the better of him and I persuade him to look at The Fax.

He picks it up with deliberation and scans the writing – not neat print, but hasty handwritten script:

Meet me in the park at sunset – all will be explained.

The girl downstairs x

Hope surges within me, but I keep it carefully hidden from Max. *It could be the perfect opportunity to kill her*, I tell him, and he thinks on this for a moment, scanning the note again and glancing out of the window towards the park. It is already evening and the dusk is hazy. Max nods and fondles the KingCobra.

"Let's go hunting," he says, and smiles the smile of a predator.

~

We are waiting in the park as the sun finally sets. I watch the sky darken and the distant sun light up a glowing halo of orange-gold, like the aura of a candle in the deadness of the night. I see the last flames disappear beyond the ragged city skyline and the stars appear, one by one, to blanket all the heavens.

Max watches as the girl downstairs walks towards us through the park.

Please, I ask him, *let me get some answers before you kill her.*

She is dressed to stun; short black skirt, long black stockings, high black heels. She wears a loose white silk shirt that only buttons halfway up, and black lace peeks through beneath it. Her dark hair is pinned up, her lips rouged, her eyes smouldering. I want to take her to Jeanie's bench and give her a thorough going-over. Even Max wants to sink his teeth in.

"You're looking better," she says softly, running her hand across my cheek. The cold after-taste of her skin makes me gasp.

"What do you want?" Max demands, folding his arms.

She smiles, showing small white teeth. "I thought this might help you."

We take the piece of paper she holds out, unfolding it to find a phone number.

"What is this?"

"The number of those people who call you all the time. I traced it through your fax machine."

It is beginning to rain. The rain is light and soft. I stare, nonplussed, as Max questions her further.

"How did you get this?"

"I work for the switchboard," she explains. "When I said I was going out for a date, I didn't mean it. I slipped back to work and pretended I'd been given a late shift. I tried to trace the calls back to their source, but the number was protected. It took *forever* to search through the database and logs, but eventually...well, that's it. That's the number."

Behind Max, I sagged, weak with relief. Not that she had found the number – *that* fact barely registered – but that she hadn't been with someone else. I hadn't been betrayed. She loved *me*!

Max folded the piece of paper and stowed it safely away. "Why are you doing this?"

"I figured you were in trouble. The gun...the fax with my picture on it...I thought...maybe...if I helped you..."

Max took a step closer. "I wouldn't kill you."

She nodded. "Something like that."

She smells *great*. She's wearing perfume, something spicy. Her skin is pale and smooth like buttermilk and I want to caress every inch of her, while Max is determining the softest part to bite.

He has caught her scent and he wants her, as much as I do. He wants to claim her, mark her, love her, consume her. He wants to make her beg for him. Then he wants to kill her.

72

The rain is growing cool; she shivers. I want to wrap my arms around her. I would give my skin to keep her warm.

"Let's go inside," Max invites her, and I feel a pang of fear as his thoughts cross my mind. He will take her, ravage her. I fight him but it is no use, he is too strong for me – and like all the others, she is captured by his gaze. He slips a strong arm around her and takes her back to his lair.

~

She is walking slowly backwards as they come through the door, her finger curling as she tempts him forwards. He seems to be following her, but appearances deceive – she doesn't know it yet but he's stalking her, and any moment he will pounce.

I am powerless to stop him. Part of me wants to save her, but the other part...the other part wants her too, and wants Max to take her. I am filled with the urge to dominate, but it is Max's lust. His insatiable, animal lust. It threatens to consume me, I can hardly fight it any more.

Max grabs her by the arms and propels her backwards, forcing her onto the sofa. Because she thinks it is a game, she does not fight – not really. Her struggling is feigned and weak, playful and tormenting. Max pins her down and tears her shirt open, growling. She bares her teeth and they lock together in a violent kiss. I cannot tear my eyes away, I'm desperate to take her and desperate to save her. Take her, protect her, take, protect, rape, protect...

She is arching her back and moaning as Max makes his marks down her neck and starts towards her breasts. She claws at his back, eyes closed in pleasure, clings to him with her legs, pulls him towards her with powerful hands.

He is drawn to her throat, the soft white curve of it, the sweet pulse of life beneath the skin. He nips at the skin and licks with a tongue that can tear meat off the bone, and feels the blood flowing just out of reach.

Suddenly her clawing hands are tearing at his shirt, trying to take it off. I barely feel him do it, but he pulls violently away.

She stares at him, wondering if this is rejection, wondering what he will do. She draws him closer again, and I feel him let her. She strokes his face and he is still, for a moment, and confused.

Her hands are gentle, *oh so gentle*, as she takes hold of his shirt – our shirt, my shirt – and pulls it over his head. He freezes, uncertain for the first time in his life. She is trying to take control. He doesn't know what to do. He has *always* dominated.

Then it is gone, lying on the floor, a crumpled heap. The shirt, his protection. He feels naked, laid bare to her eyes – and it is not only his body exposed, it is something deep within him, something that has never surfaced in Max before. Not since Geneva…

She runs her hands up his arms, over the gentle ripple of his muscles. She tightens her grip and pulls him towards her, down towards her, and he resists a little; but only a little.

And she kisses him, so softly, so gently, that Max – Max, who has conquered a thousand women, Max who is afraid of nothing and no-one, Max who feels only animal lust and cannot conceive of love – loses a little of himself to that kiss, and is powerless to stop her doing what she is doing to him.

Her hands roam, caressing his shoulders, teasing the healing bruises that have become his through my weakness, making him gasp and wince and throb all the more for her.

And her hands find his back, and the landscape of his body changes. He tries to pull away again, but she holds fast to him, delicate fingers exploring the scarred terrain.

Max can stand no more. The lust, the need, the fear…they are wolves, they harass him, they threaten to undo him. He is no longer in control. He is being exploited. He can't stand it. He is terrified.

He stumbles away, leaving her lying on the sofa, staring at him. He is naked to her dark eyes, a victim to her animal smile.

She is curious and she rises, walks to him, reaches for him. He slaps her hands away, tries to hit her. He can't. For the first time in his life, Max cannot raise his hand. He sees something in her eyes that is even more…animal, than he.

She reaches out again, and this time he does not move. He is torn with indecision and frozen with fear – fear that she will find *him*. Fear that she will find out who we really are and expose the past we have spent so long escaping.

Her hands are cool silk as they glide over our skin. Without even trying, they push away our defences. They leave us clothed yet render us naked. They are like eyes, seeing everything we have and seeing past the walls we have built so high. They explore our body, they are at our back again, and they see what we cannot, but what we know is there – the scars that hold such terrible memories in their ridges and valleys and hills. She has breached our last defence; the wall is ready to tumble.

Like a floodgate opening, pressed against her body, held in her hands, Max begins to cry. The tears spill from his blue-green eyes, dampen her dark hair, and his great body heaves with silent sobs. He cannot help it, neither of us can. We clutch her to our body, her face resting against our chest, her arms wrapped around us, tight, so tight, so safe. And we cry, because we have never cried before.

Max is vulnerable, Max is weak, Max is waking to the world and remembering who he is; *who I am*. The things we have been through, the reason he has always had to be so strong. Max is spilling Geneva, crying for China, and remembering those dark cells, those sharp blades, and I feel the pain at last subside. I feel Max slowly slip away. Peaceful, quiet, going, gone. And I…I am free.

66: Stage Four – Tracing the Target

This time, she is sleeping in my arms when I wake. It takes me a few moments to remember last night, but her presence in my bed, and the absence of Max inside my head, are enough to confirm that something miraculous has happened. I feel warm, happy, at peace, complete. I could not ask for anything more.

I slip away as the sleeper sleeps, make breakfast in the kitchen. There is an ancient radio that has not sung for ten years; I plug it in, switch it on, tune the vicious fuzz and suddenly the room is filled with music. I am surprised by violin music, sweet as can be, spiralling and soaring and taking me with it. It is the most beautiful thing I have ever heard, and it lifts me until I am smiling and crying all at once.

I brew tea and fry bread and cook sausages and scramble eggs to the violin's voice, then think that maybe she would like something else, so I toast some toast and unpack the blueberry jam that fell on my foot (was it really only yesterday that I got angry over something so insignificant?), and pour some orange juice and stick a slice of orange on the side of the glass. I empty the tinned apricots right beside the chopped bananas. I warm the brioche and scour the cupboards for something else…something red…like strawberry jam. For absolutely no reason at all, I draw a jammy red heart right on top of each soft brioche.

There is something missing. Checking she is still asleep, I slip into jeans and a shirt and run outside to the park.

I pick daffodils, pansies, wild roses, dandelions, buttercups, a few pretty-looking purple thistle-heads. I bring them back inside and spread them on the tray, right beside the food. There. Am most romantic bloke in the world.

She seems to think so too, because she takes a sip of tea, smiles, and before she can even touch her painted brioche she has thrown me on the bed and kissed me all over.

I can only grin like an idiot and stare at the ceiling, and think *how in the world have I done without this every day of my life?*

We shower together, squashed like two pearls in a shell. Slimy and wet, elbowing each other as we try to wash our hair. It turns out that it's easier to wash each other's hair, so we do. Then she pushes me against the cold tiles, and claims me with a bruising kiss.

We get out. "I don't have work 'til late," she tells me, as she towels her hair dry.

I am sitting on the side of the bath, watching her breasts jiggle as she rubs herself dry. She is simply the most beautiful thing I have ever seen, and I'm not *really* listening as she talks.

"Hey, pervert," she says, and kicks my shin. But she is smiling. "I said, I'm not working 'til later."

I nod and ask why.

"Late shift. Money's better." She shrugs, and her breasts jiggle some more. They are captivating. I am a snake, they are the piper's music, and I feel myself rise in response.

"I thought we could phone that number," she said. "Better get it done sooner rather than later."

I shiver as I remember Mission 66. But she's right – I have to phone THEM. I have to find out what's going on. But I won't tell THEM about this. THEY don't have to know.

When we are dried and dressed, I find the piece of paper she gave to Max last night. Last night seems so long ago; I was a different person, then.

I dial the number into the phone. She nods reassurance and I smile and turn away from her as someone answers; it is The Voice.

"Who is this?" THEY demand. "How did you get this number?"

It's me. You know me. It's about Mission 66.

"Aah."

There is no note of surprise – I wonder if THEY have known all along that I would be in contact over this one.

Why her, I ask THEM. *Why is* she *The Target?*

"You aren't supposed to ask questions," THEY tell me.

But I persist.

I have never questioned you before, but I'm questioning you now. Tell me why you chose her. What has she done to deserve a Mission File?

"She has done nothing."

Then, why...

"You should be asking yourself that. It was you, after all, that initiated contact." There is a pause. "Or, perhaps you should ask Jeremiah."

I let the silence hang – not because I want to, but because I can't think of anything to say. Jeremiah? What has Jeremiah got to do with this? He left after The Shot was fired…

"Is that all?"

No, I…

"You will complete your Mission, under whatever guise you choose, or your contract will be terminated. Do you understand me? Now, don't ever phone this number again."

Then there was silence, the dead tone.

"Well?" she asked, as I put the phone down. "What did they say?"

How could I tell this beautiful girl that unless I carried out The Mission, I would be killed?

I swallowed hard, and smiled.

Let's go for a walk.

~

I always familiarise myself with The Target, whether it be by looking at his Files or following him around as he goes about his day. It isn't easy to follow the ones with bodyguards and body-doubles to throw potential assassins off the scent. These I watch from a distance, and learn about through their profiles – like I did with Mission 65.

Whatever my methods, I always take the time to learn about The Target before The Shot. It helps me to predict their movements, their reactions, even the way they will die.

So now I am learning about the girl downstairs. Familiarising myself with her. Only, unlike all the others, she is telling me willingly.

We are sat in the park, not on Jeanie's bench because two children are kneeling on it and spitting over the backrest into a puddle caused by last night's rain.

It is warm, like summer, and she's wearing a long yellow dress with no sleeves, and flat white sandals with big pink flowers on them. She has a rose stuck through her hair at an angle – one I picked for her this morning. She looks a little tanned, and tells me she goes to the gym.

We bought crêpe pancakes at the stand on the corner. She has chocolate and fudge sauce and marshmallows in hers. I have cheese. She screws up her face as she watches me eat, and shudders as she smiles because 'there's *so* much fat in cheese'.

I don't care. And besides, I tell her, how much fat does she think is in chocolate and fudge sauce and marshmallows?

"*And* chocolate ice cream," she says, licking the chocolate sauce as it dribbles darkly out of the sides. "It's not the same thing, anyway. You can't *see* the fat in chocolate. It doesn't count."

She finishes and licks her fingers and wipes them down my shirt with a wicked grin.

"I used to eat chocolate sauce from a jar with a spoon when I was little," she tells me.

I smile and am about to say, *I eat mayonnaise like that*, when I realise that was Jeremiah's thing, not mine.

I hate mayonnaise. I hate Jeremiah. I must talk to him later and find out what THEY meant.

She is playing with the bracelet she always wears, silver with tiny charms; a horse, an elephant, a music box. I know the elephant well, for it attacked me with its tiny tusks last night.

"I get these from my friends and family every birthday," she explains, seeing me looking at the bracelet. She touches each tiny charm with care. "One from everyone I love. The music box is from my brother, the horse is from my mum. This," and she picks up the delicate silver heart, "This was from my first boyfriend. He gave it to me when I turned twenty, along with a ring."

She shows me the slender gold band with its beautiful diamond – the only charm on her bracelet that isn't silver.

"He wanted me to marry him." Tears fill her eyes. She sighs and looks away. "Then he was killed."

I put my arm around her shoulders and press her to my chest. *I'm so sorry,* I tell her. *How did he die?*

"He was a waiter," she said. "One night he tripped on a lady's dress and fell on his tray of salmon en croutes. A pastry fork went right through his heart."

She wiped her eyes with a cocked forefinger. "I can't eat en croutes now – they only remind me of him."

She told me about her childhood, and how she had learned early on to look after herself. Her mother worked as a seamstress and her father left when she was three and turned up periodically when he was drunk or penniless to beg a place to sleep or a loan, claiming he was sorry he had ever left.

She hadn't been able to afford college, so went on to work with her mother for a couple of years before finding work as a switchboard operator. She was deft-handed and fast, and developed something of a reputation in the switchboard-world. A large company got wind and picked her up, giving her training and a respectable salary, on which she now supports herself and her mother.

"I was assessed by MI6, too," she whispers, squeezing my hand, "But I'm not supposed to tell anyone, so don't go spreading it around."

What happened? I asked.

"I didn't fit the profile. You have to fit a certain profile, and I just wasn't it. But I picked up some of the training, anyway – that's how I knew how to trace that number."

I am suitably impressed.

"So, tell me about you," she says, suddenly. "You have, like, a personality disorder, don't you?"

I smile at her and kiss her forehead.

Something like that, I said.

~

In truth, there is little of me that I remember, or wish to. My childhood is a blur, a confusion of other people's lives. I remember Max's foster homes and Jeremiah's valley farm and Harry's parents' divorce and Ned's abuse with such clarity that each experience could be my own. But none of them really are, I think.

I don't like going back to my past. Any further back than that first Mission is mine-studded territory and I would much rather give it all a wide berth. *This* is my life now, it is what I make it and I have made it this. I have sixty-five Missions to my various names, have amassed a quite reasonable sum of money and have met a girl with whom I would like to spend the rest of my days (so long as I don't kill her first).

But I have nightmares, sometimes.

I dream of the ocean, though I'm sure I've never been to sea. I dream I'm far out on the water, adrift without a life vest or a boat. I can't see the shore in any direction and a storm is gathering over my head. The sky is growing almost black, the clouds so close they try to push me under, and beneath me is a stretch of water so fathomless and dark that I tremble to think what is swimming about my legs.

Other times my dreams are more specific; I dream I am back in Geneva, only it is me instead of Max they have strapped to a table. Or I am in China, and hanging upside down by my ankles as they drip water into my face for days upon days without end.

These tortures last aeons before I wake, and when I do I'm bathed in sweat and gasping for breath, and must run to the kitchen and rattle the pans and cups to convince myself that *this* is real, and not the dreams.

I haven't had those nightmares for a while now, I realise. Not since I met her.

We don't leave the park until this little patch of world has grown dark and cool again. I barely notice time when she's around; somehow we have spent the whole day here, and in bed. She tells me she must go to work soon. I watch solemnly, funereally, as she stands on the pavement and hails a car. She waves to me as she climbs in, then is driven out of my sight.

I feel alone again without her, though I know that I am not, and I resolve to talk to Jeremiah, to find out where he was the night I was attacked.

~

Jeremiah is a most difficult person to trace. He is elusive and solitary, and can hide far better than any giraffe behind a tall tree. He acts like a child playing hide-and-seek, laughing at me as I pounce only to discover he's moved on and all that's in my hands is cold and empty air.

But I do reason with him, and soon he is sitting on my sofa. He wants a banana milkshake.

I have none, I tell him. *Why did you leave me the night I was attacked? Why didn't you help me?*

He smiles at me, casually.

"Did you need my help? You should have asked. I thought you had it all under control."

Under control? I got beaten half to death!

"But you didn't die, did you? You're here, aren't you?"

No thanks to you. What did THEY mean about initiating contact?

"With the girl downstairs? Oh, I sent you to her."

WHY?

"You said it yourself, they beat you half to death. I wasn't going to stand by and see you bleed your sorry self all over the park, was I? All the flowers would have come up red next summer."

Why did you send me to her*? Why did you have to involve her in all this?*

Jeremiah leaned forward and looked me right in the eyes. "You've been playing this one-man-band for *far* too long, my friend. I just put a hole in your drum."

~

"Everybody at work's still talking about it," she tells me, returning late – or rather, early – and slipping into bed. She doesn't even bother taking off her make-up – just steps out of her clothes and shakes her hair loose and slips between the sheets.

She is icy-cold against my bed-warm body, and she curls around me to steal my heat. She smells like people and outside and an office noisy with the rapid-fire clack-clack-clack of long nails on keyboards keys, and of vanilla musk in the secret corners of her.

Talking about what?

"That man, the one who got shot. The police think it was a sniper."

I nod and murmur as she tells me about it, then groan happily as she kneads the knots away from me and talks some more. Her voice becomes a background drone, a warm buzz to lull me asleep. When I wake, some time before dawn, she is cuddled up to me, snoring gently in my ear.

I lay awake and stare at the ceiling. I remember distantly that she told me the police were going door-to-door in the hope someone had witnessed *something*. They will come to my door, eventually, and I will have to tell them the truth.

I was not there.

Wok a Nice Policeman

She has gone to work again. An early shift following a late shift is just cruel, she says, though her voice is light and she doesn't seem ruffled, and I say nothing but grow to loathe her work as a manifest evil. She might as well be on Pluto or Saturn, or one of Jupiter's moons – Ganymede, perhaps – for I am as desolate in her absence as I would be in her death.

What did I *do* before I knew her? What solitary muse occupied my lonely hours?

Ah, the Parker-Hale. I fetch it from its case and lovingly caress its every glinting surface.

It has evoked mixed feelings in me, this possession, since I first glimpsed it through the tangle of Somalia's savannah thorn bushes, slung across the chest and shoulder of a storm-skinned figure lying prone on the parched ground.

The man was as dead as nailed dormice. His immobile face was a broad, flat black plain, the skin ashy and smooth and slick like oil. The unseeing eyes, riveted to the sky in an expression of wondrous fear, were soft brown, bright white, and filled with such sadness that for a moment I was overcome.

As strong as was my instinct to attempt a burial, I let him be. There were no wounds on his body, saved a tiny, swollen bite on his left wrist.

He seemed so peaceful, in retrospect, that it would have been a pity to spoil his repose.

I took the Parker-Hale and nothing else, and left him to the swift workings of the vultures and the dogs.

The rifle survived, undetected, through a dozen customs checks, and despite one or two exhilarating and terrifying encounters with Authority, who we thwarted narrowly and with great imagination (brandishing the all-important Papers helped, though not enough can be said for the effectiveness of a little confidence and grovelling), we made it safely home.

We have weathered many seasons, it and I, ever since that *very first shot*, but as with any great friend, we have fought and fallen out, and reconciled our differences time and again. I have thrown it down in abject misery and loathed it with all my soul, and I have turned to it when all else seemed in darkness and it offered me the only hope in all my tortured world. Even, on the very odd occasions, it has given me great joy, and brought a smile to my knotted face: stalking through the Congo in search of vengeance from a hated foe; and, finding that foe, vanquishing him swiftly and simply with a soft caress.

A knocking came at my door. Hands full, as they were, of dismembered Parker-Hale, I could only snap my head towards the sound and freeze, stare, hold my breath and wait. The cold metal in my hands was as rigid and unmoving as my body. We waited, it and I, until the knocking came again, and a voice with it across the distance travelled;

"Sir? It's the police. Can we have a word?"

I came unglued and began to move, with practised and automatic fluidity. The Parker-Hale's case was in the kitchen; no time to fetch it, unless I wished to arouse their suspicion. I laid the pieces of the rifle down on the carpet and carefully pushed them underneath the sofa.

Coming, I call, and pet the Glock concealed beneath my shirt.

I open the door.

Two policemen, uniformly tall and blue-eyed, stand patiently outside. They glance at one another upon seeing my face; I do not hesitate, and bid them, *please come in,* and shut the door behind.

They sit on my sofa and I take a seat in the chair. They sit above evidence every bit as incriminating beneath their buttocks as a body. They clasp their hands and lean forward, resting elbows on their thighs. I smile. *Would they like a cup of tea?*

"Tea would be very nice, thank you," says one.

"No, thank you," says the second. "Sir, we haven't come to use your kettle, we've come to ask you some questions. Would you mind?"

Not at all, not at all. Ask away, say I.

"Where were you on the night of the sixteenth, sir?"

At home, I think. I don't really recall.

"You may have heard on the news…"

I don't have a television.

"Well, you may have read it in the paper, then…"

I don't buy the paper, I'm afraid.

"It was only on Saturday, sir," says the first, impatiently.

"Regardless of whether you know about it or not, sir," interjects the second, "A man was murdered not far from here on the sixteenth. We are questioning everyone in the vicinity in case they witnessed anything that day and haven't yet spoken out about what they saw, for whatever reason. A number of people so far have volunteered information that was previously withheld. Would you know anything of this occurrence, sir?"

Of the murder? Or of the witnesses volunteering information?

"Of the murder, if you please."

No, I'm afraid not.

"Nothing at all?"

Not a thing.

"You see, we have been informed that a scuffle occurred in the park opposite on the night of the sixteenth, and the victim was seen seeking shelter in this building. Call it police intuition, if you will, but I have the feeling that this victim knows something about the murder. You see, the two assailants match the description of two gentlemen who were spotted near the scene of the murder just a few minutes earlier."

Yes, that does seem coincidental, doesn't it? But, I'm afraid I really can't help you there, officer. You see, I was at home all day.

"You're certain of that, sir? A moment ago you said you couldn't really recall."

Yes, but as the sixteenth was only Saturday, I have remembered.

"I see. And do you have any witnesses to your being at home all day?"

No, none. But you could try asking the other occupants of this building. They will not have seen me, of that I am carefully confident. They don't care what goes on outside these walls, or inside them either, often. I have come to value the uncaring discretion of my neighbours.

"Thank you, we will. Why is it that you were at home on Saturday, sir? What were you doing all day?"

"With no television," threw in the first.

Oh, you know. This and that. Sleeping, mostly. My work requires that strange hours be committed to it.

"And what *is* your job, if I may ask?"

I am a squirrel collector.

"A…squirrel collector?"

Yes, mostly. Squirrels, pigeons, hedgehogs, badgers, the occasional fox or owl.

"Ah, road kill."

Yes. Night is the best time to do my work, you see. When they're fresh.

"How morbid."

Yes it is. Would you like that cup of tea?

"Yes, please," says the first.

"No, no thanks," the second interrupts. "He wouldn't."

"Yes I would."

"No, you wouldn't."

"Actually, I…"

"Actually, we must be going." The second silences the first with a glare.

I show them to the door.

"May I ask, sir," says the second, stopping in the doorway and turning back to me, "How you came to be so…discoloured?"

I smile, crookedly.

I was fallen on.

"Fallen on? By whom?"

By what.

"Beg pardon?"

By what. It was a box.

"A box?"

A box. A box fell on me.

"A box fell on you?"

A cardboard box.

"A cardboard box…" and the policeman points at my face, whose misshapen prominences and sorry, swollen recesses are a quilt of colour, "…did that?"

Yes. Well, no. It was really more the pan that fell out of the box.

"A pan fell out of the box…onto your face?"

Oh, no. It fell on my head. Stunned me, just a little bit. It was the others… and I indicate the crowbar-bump, the wonky nose, the blackened eyes and crooked smile …*that did this.*

He nods slowly. "The others? How many others?"

Oh, no more than twenty, I'd say. Though, I really stopped counting after the first five.

"I see. And these were…frying pans? Or saucepans?"

Oh, no. Woks.

"Woks? Twenty woks. Huh. You must really like Chinese, huh?"

I grimace lopsidedly. *Not any more.*

The Wind and the Swan

The fax machine drools paper onto the carpet.

"Oh goody," says Jeremiah, nimble fingers stretching and cracking and twitching with eagerness as he grabs The Fax before I can stop him. "I want something to do." He sounds petulant. "I'm *bored*."

Good, I say, *I'm glad you're bored. Now shut up and leave me alone.*

"Oh, I don't think so. This is *far* too interesting."

He scans the first page and laughs; a cultured, restrained, gentle-sounding laugh.

I loathe his laugh – it echoes too familiarly, in its feminine softness, of *her* laugh, and I shudder that so beautiful a sound could come from so hated a mouth as his.

The Fax is about *her*. Her life – so far – is succinctly rounded down to a few mere bullets on a page. (I wonder how many bullets would summarise *my* life – in some senses, many, but in others very few.)

Education:
- John Edmond Primary
- John Edmond South Upper Girls' School

Employment:
- Newspaper delivery (7 months)
- Babysitting (2 months)
- Trainee seamstress (2 years 4 months)
- Waitress (4 months)
- Switchboard operator (7 years to present)

Criminal record:

- 4 parking tickets
- 1 speeding fine
- Violent behaviour at anti-nuclear-weapons protest rally (leading to arrest and overnight stint at local police station)
- Resisting arrest at (above) anti-nuclear-weapons protest rally (leading to £150 fine and verbal warning)
- Indecent exposure at (above) anti-nuclear-weapons protest rally (leading to arrest and chilblains)
- Charged with suspected possession of cocaine (arrested, but later released without charge when found merely to be in possession of unnatural quantities of sherbet dib-dabs)

I stared at the words for the longest time, seeing in them nothing – *not a thing* – that should make me want to kill her. Why would THEY send me this?

"You might not want to kill her," Jeremiah said, "But this sure as Hell makes me."

Why?

"Because. She's too good."

I didn't answer, but remembered what I'd thought when first meeting Jeremiah.

I'm sure he's not all good... No-one's all good. He'll show me his dark side sooner or later.

"I can hear what you're thinking," he says.

Piss off, I say back.

Bored, he leaves me alone for a little while. I sit on the sofa and stare through the glass at the park, and know that another pair of eyes is watching this same scene; the same wind-ruffled trees, the same rough, rippled pond.

The same neat swans, their white sails tucked away lest the wind pick them up and carry them far off. The same children playing, careless of the cold, on a green that is greener against the red of their cheeks.

I wonder just how much the old man saw that night, when two shadows fell upon me and fed my blood to the thirsty ground. I wonder if he saw, with his old eyes, the faces of the men who drove their shoes into my soft body; or if he saw the face of the victim, and if so why he did not speak.

On the pond, a swan unfurls its vast white wings and is plucked at by the wind. It is pulled a little way up, out of the water, just so the tops of its legs are visible; part of me (the childish part) wants to see it blush and try to cover its legs with its wings, but instead it catches the wind and seems almost to stand upon the water, graceful neck extended forwards and skywards, its every feather contemplating flight.

I stare and freeze, locked in vicarious battle. The urge to fly is vast, even though flight in such wind could prove fatal, if smashed against a tree or swept into the road. The soft safety of the water stretches below, at the touch of a webbed foot, and just for a moment the swan seems to sink back down into its wet embrace.

But just before it does, it spreads its wings that little bit further – almost a stretch, almost accompanied by a yawn, that says, *this doesn't frighten me, I am stronger than the wind* – and they are pulled taut like a sail.

Then the wings fold, the swan settles, and all is still once more. The vicious gusts pass, the swan's feathers barely ruffled. But in its black eye, the challenge of the wild remains.

The wind and the swan will meet again, and next time the swan will win.

He mustn't have seen, I reason, and turn away from the window. The old man, he mustn't have seen my face that night.

It would have been too dark.

NOT Taking The Shot:
An Entirely New Stage of The Game

She will be back from work, soon; I am brushing my teeth in preparation.

What are you smiling at? I ask, as Jeremiah grins from the mirror. His white teeth highlight a tan I would burn to death receiving.

"I am not smiling, brother," he says, "I am laughing. Laughing at you. You are so pathetic."

Go away, I tell him, *I'm no brother of yours.*

"We are all children of God, and joined in brotherhood beneath His gaze."

Tell that to the man you murdered. Tell that to his children.

Jeremiah cocks his head, puppy-like, and tuts chidingly. "Tch, tch. You simply can't admit responsibility, can you? You have lost sight of The Cause."

What do you want? I ask, angry now. I want to brush my teeth in peace.

"I want what every man wants, drummer-boy – absolution. Absolution in the eyes of God."

I don't want absolution.

"Oh but you do. Deep down, you really do. It's what makes you so easy to play with. You are my *toy*, I can make you do *anything*."

I stab my toothbrush toward the mirror. *You can't make me stop loving her.*

"That's true. Love seems to be the one thing He doesn't begrudge us." He smiles hungrily. "But I can make you *hurt* her."

This time the toothbrush makes contact with the mirror, leaving bristles and paste smeared on the glass.

Leave her out of this. Why do you want to hurt her so much?

"Because I can. Because hurting her hurts *you*. I loathe you, you and your disgusting little world. I want cleanliness, sterility. I want the sterile emptiness of death."

You want me dead, so you lead me to a girl? How clever you are, Jeremiah, I mock. *How very clever.*

He raised his hands, martyr-like, and cast his eyes toward the ceiling.

"And the Lord said, 'I will completely destroy them and make them an object of horror and scorn, and everlasting ruin.'"

You fancy yourself as something of a preacher.

"Not a preacher, o small minded one. I am a messenger of Our Lord."

Of course you are.

"Of course I am. What else would I be?"

A psychopath.

"Aah, yes. But what would that make you, dear drummer-boy? You are what I am, and what I create, and what I control. You are a servant unto Our Lord, and Our Lord resides in me. Now, heed my wise words and clean that crap off the mirror."

I was about to reply, when a dribble of toothpaste slithered down my stubbled chin, snaking between the bristles, and I struck upon the most fantastic of ideas. *You really think you're God, Jeremiah?*

"Of course I am." He smiled smugly, but his eyes shifted nervously to our face. "Stop dribbling – you look like an imbecile."

I thought you were God? So make me stop.

I am a genius! *This* was an idea *far* more worthy of intellectual admiration than the epiphany I had the day I shot myself in the foot. Fortunately I have left the Glock in the living room, because this level of sagacity calls for far greater wounding.

Jeremiah is growing more and more agitated. His neat, dark brows furrow at the sight of the dribbling toothpaste. He is shifting from foot to foot as the mouth-warm liquid oozes between my teeth and caresses my chin and plops into the sink, splattering the enamel.

Getting to you, am I? I enquire, mildly, sounding more confident than I feel. *Or does God treat His children with patience and tolerance?*

"Stop it!" Jeremiah yells, and I promptly wipe the back of my hand across my mouth. Toothpaste stains my cheek white. I reach into the cupboard and pull out a can of shaving gel. Jeremiah grips his hair and clenches his teeth in tortured anticipation as I point the can deliberately at the wall and press.

White foam shoots out at speed and expands as it hits the damp plaster, coating ribbons of the bathroom wall with delicious, elicit mess. This is better than graffiti, I think, and wonder why men the world over only shave with this stuff. Jeremiah cringes and curses as I stand back to admire my handiwork.

Bacon sandwich, I have written, in childish, melting swirls. *Fat on.*

Jeremiah is writhing, disgust and shame growing from mental torment to physical violation. The smear of dripping foam upon the rotting plaster is quite enough alone to unnerve him; but the words themselves and the images they conjure up threaten his sanity. He implores me to quit my workings, but I am by now bent upon one aim; Jeremiah must go.

"Stop!" he shouts, teeth jittering, as I rub our naked toes into the mouldy corner of carpet where the shower has leaked and turned the fibres greenish-black. He squirms with revulsion and tries to drag me back, but for once my determination is stronger than his pedant philosophies. I force him to his knees and drive his long, lean, piano-playing fingers into the gunge.

"Stop it!" he shrieks, yanking me so forcibly away that we stagger up and back and crash resoundingly against the door, and spill into the apartment like sloshed milk.

I stumble into the kitchen, dragging him almost by the hair, and propel us immediately to the sink. I plunge our hands into the backlog of greasy dishwater.

He flounders like a fish on land, eyes goggle-wide and mouth opening and closing as if to suck in air – though I know he is searching for the words with which to curse me, and the breath with which to voice his horror.

Jeremiah. Cool, calm, sophisticated Jeremiah, who could draw in curious women like cats to the cream, whose dove-white smile spoke of freedom and whose long giraffe legs were vehicles on which to evade the consequences.

Jeremiah, on the brink of madness at the sight of mess.

How it made me laugh.

I pity the poor girl that falls to your charms, Jerry.

"I pity the girl who's fallen to yours," he sneers back, snatching his hands from the water and clutching tight to the side of the sink to still the shaking of his limbs. "You'll shoot her in the end. You'll be the downfall of your own little Jerusalem!"

I feel anger boil inside me and propel him to the fridge, and grab the first thing that comes to hand; that bottle of sour milk.

"Throw it away!" he cries, trying to snatch it from me.

Not a chance. It's not that *old; here, smell it.*

"Get it away from me!"

Go on, just a sniff. Here, I'll do it.

"No! Don't...blooooooaargh!"

Oh, don't be such a baby. Look, I don't feel sick.

But, of course, I do. I feel like following Jeremiah's example and committing my breakfast to the depths of the greasy sink-sea. I want to open wide the windows and empty the bottle's offensive lumpy contents down upon the heads of passers-by.

I want to run to the girl downstairs and bury myself in her sweet-smelling flesh.

But I persevere. For the sake of her, I persevere. I must drive Jeremiah away. If I don't, without Max, *he* will take on Mission 66, and that must not be allowed.

I force the milk to my lips and take a sip, cringing and shuddering and gagging and retching, and all the while Jeremiah is squirming in agony more intense and deep-rooted than my mere physical revulsions; his fears are manifested psychologically, tapering back to a childhood founded on sterility and rooted in the abject dread of germs, coughs, colds, sniffles, fever, infection, dust, dirt, grime, and all the other little niceties of life.

But while I could, in a more understanding frame of mind, sympathise deeply with such a fear (having handled Harry in a restaurant when his drink came with a slice of orange; having forced Robert into a room full of people, only to have him bounce off the walls and run for the nearest cyber-café), now is not my most sympathetic moment.

And, besides, I liked Robert, with his kind heart and gentle ways.

I related to Harry; his jokes made me laugh.

I can find *nothing* likeable about Jeremiah, therefore I have no reason to try and understand him. He is arrogant, supercilious, egotistical, possibly a little psychotic, and I do not sympathise even a little bit.

And, with that conclusion armed, I proceed again to the fridge and pull out of it – shelf by shelf – every scrap of food.

Half a tin of baked beans, trimmed with white fur; open pack of bacon rashers, greener than they should be; out-of-date fromage frais; wrinkly red tomatoes; yellow cucumber marinating in its own juices; several half-eaten apples (a trait of Robert's I have been unable to shake); wilting lettuce still in its cellophane; a fuzzy block of *very* mature cheese; and, of course, a jar of mayonnaise.

Because Jeremiah *loves* mayonnaise.

I have no hesitation at all – no question in my mind – about what I will do with so much wasted food.

Jeremiah would hate to see it wasted, and besides, it won't all fit in the bin. I start with the mayonnaise, the food Jeremiah eats right from the jar. I find a spoon.

Hungry, Jerr? I ask, and shove a laden tablespoon down his throat.

We get through the jar – *the whole jar.* It isn't off, but it's not exactly pleasant either. So much mayonnaise eaten on its own takes on a sour, stomach-churning quality. *I can certainly feel* your *stomach churning, Jerr. Aren't you enjoying this?*

I grab a plate and tip the mouldy beans and geriatric tomatoes onto it in a gloopy, rancid pile. Jeremiah is clawing at his throat and pounding the floor with weakening feet as I pluck a spatula from the sink (unwashed) and use it to cram this sorry-looking hash-up between his irritatingly white teeth, followed swiftly by the *last inch* of orange juice, right out of the carton.

It's not iced coffee, that's for sure, I say, as he sprawls to his knees and vomits in the most undignified manner.

I haul him up and make him eat the eight-pack of fromage frais I bought in a moment of culinary experimentation; no spoon, this time, but with his fingers – his long, piano-playing fingers that scrape the bottom of the pot and all around the sides like they were made with the specific intent of scraping fromage frais pots clean. He cries and retches and spits surprisingly inventive curses, but I make him finish *every...last...one.*

The browning apples and bitter, oozing lettuce leaves have gone, too, chased down by chunks of veteran cheddar. But even I don't have the courage to look towards the yellow cucumber (which really does its stuff to convince me of its 96.3% water content), because my legs are already jelly and my insides feel like a washing machine drum on spin cycle.

Just be glad I've not resorted to the liquorice laces yet, I say, as Jeremiah whinges and whines – on the verge, I think, of complete nervous collapse – and begs me to stop.

He is so fragile, so frail, as I haul him by the scruff to his knees and make him chew the raw bacon rashers, that it is easy to forget he has no conscience, and that he would gladly put a hole in the woman I love, just for money.

"Not even...for money," he splutters, with the last ounce of his stubborn strength. "I'd kill her for free."

I think it must have been a few seconds later that she came in (I had given her a key), because I jumped then at her gasp of shock as she laid eyes on me, on my knees on the kitchen floor, baked beans clinging to my hair and yoghurt plastering my face; one hand clawing at the fridge, the other ramming a foot-long soggy yellow cucumber into my mouth and down my throat, and my whole body shuddering with wretched convulsions.

"What are you *doing*?" she cried, hand fluttering to her mouth like that frightened moth I saw so many moons ago.

I stared, gagged and withdrew the cucumber, and wiped my mouth on my sleeve.

"Getting rid of some things I didn't want," I said.

"Are they gone?" she ventured.

I looked about me at the devastation and felt – aside from the most god-awfully appalling stomach ache – a strange sense of calm.

"Yes," I said, "I think they're gone."

Strange how she loves me, when I seem to spend fifty percent of our time together being sick on her floor or on mine.

Chinese Food and Photographs

I showed her The Fax, with the details of her life bulleted in black blood; she only laughed, and often cringed, as she read the words and remembered her past.

"I can't believe they thought it was drugs," she blushes, cheeks and neck rose-pink. "I should have false teeth by now, I ate so much sherbet when I was a kid."

We eat the Sherbet Fountains I bought – her with relish, me with difficulty but also with a sense of satisfaction – and I make the liquorice last and last, and think how much I am enjoying it, *simply* because I know Jeremiah hates it. Or would hate it, if he was here – but he's not, and I am glad.

She wants to spend the rest of the night watching soppy films and eating, but we've no food left between us, what with her haphazard shopping habits and the contents of my fridge being strewn across the kitchen floor, and so we agree on takeaway.

We rent two films and buy Chinese from a shop on the corner; egg fried rice, chicken wontons, prawn toast, mushroom noodles, beef in oyster sauce, stir-fried vegetables and bean-sprouts, chips with curry sauce. We decide against the duck.

"It might be related to our park ducks," she points out. "Brother and sister, or distant cousins, at least."

We trek home, tormented by the mouth-watering smells leaking from our hot boxes. The night is unexpectedly chilly, so we cradle the boxes like babies to our chests.

The film flickers in the darkness as we cuddle up on her sofa and eat. I am surprisingly hungry, to say I ate the contents of my kitchen only an hour or two ago (but then, I did return most of it after drinking two glasses of salt water at her request).

She is a bottomless pit. Having polished off the Chinese, she consumes (at alarming speed) a bag of toffee popcorn, a tub of Ben and Jerry's, and several white mice. I help her, of course, but only a little.

Then she falls asleep halfway through Harry meeting Sally, and I must watch Meg Ryan orgasm in the café alone.

~

The beautiful sleeper; I leave her on the sofa, clear away our mess and go to her room.

It is not the first time I have been in here (our lovemaking carries us to every room on both floors) but it is the first time I have seen it in the dark; she insists on having a light on, just so she can watch my face.

The bed is neatly made-up, the corners squared and tucked under with military precision. I was surprised by this at first; I would not have thought to accuse her of being neat.

Propped against the lace-edged pillows are a lamb and a bear, one naked and the other wearing a blue checked shirt. In the bear's brown face, one eye is glass, the other is missing. The glass eye wonders what I am doing, intruding here.

On her bedside table is a pile of books, each as thick as a rugby-player's thigh. Romance novels, adventure novels, horror novels; each spine crumpled, each page dog-eared and well loved, and the print faded with reading. A half-full glass of water, some hand lotion, a hairbrush, a square box of purple tissues, a magazine, hair pins, framed pictures of her mother the seamstress, of her brother in uniform, of her cousin who she says is more like her sister.

I go to her wardrobe. Her clothes (mostly hung, some crumpled unceremoniously on the floor) smell just of her; I press my face to them and breathe her in.

There are boxes at the bottom of the wardrobe. I pick out one and divest it of its shoes. I rest it on the bed and into it carefully place each of her framed pictures.

I go about the room and find the things I think she'd like to save, and put them one by one into the box. The most battered-looking books, some CDs, a slim bottle of perfume that smells like vanilla, letters from her mother, the cuddly lamb and bear, a painting from her niece, a china mask from a trip to Italy, some certificates, two fat photo albums.

I sit on the bed and flick through the stiff pages of an album. There are pictures of her childhood, though few, and more of her young adulthood. Holding hands at the seafront with the boyfriend she loved and lost; dressed up with friends for a night out; on holiday with her cousin's family (husband, two angelic children, a picaresque villa on six combed acres in Lamia); modelling a dress her mother made, whilst her mother looks proudly on.

I sit and stare at the life I am attached to, yet so very distant from. I have never met the mother she loves, the cousin she adores, the dogs that talk to sheep, the friends she grew up with. I have never taken a photo of her, nor given her one of me. Not that I should have any of myself; but I do.

I have never known a childhood such as hers.

Sadness sweeps across me like a wind. I finish packing the box and put it at the end of her bed. I go back to the sofa and wake her gently.

She murmurs and opens sleepy eyes, then rubs fists into them as a child would, only with more mascara. She smiles and pulls me in for a kiss. I let her, but don't let it last too long.

I need you to do something for me, I say, and take her hand in mine. *I need you to leave.*

"Um, it's my flat," she jokes. "You leave."

I tell her I am serious, and this is important. A matter of life or death. I apologise for the cliché.

She sits up, wide awake now. The jeans she has changed into are unbuttoned from her earlier indulgence, and I almost smile at the sight of her soft little belly.

"What is it?" she says, "Why do I have to leave?"

I need you to pack a few things – the things you want to keep hold of, but not too much. There's something I have to do, and I don't want you to get hurt.

She listens to me steadily. "Will you be okay?"

Of course I will. I'll be fine. Will you promise me you'll go? In the morning?

She falters, but only for a second – because she is stronger than a thousand bullet-proof vests. Because she knows that this is serious, and because she sees in my eyes that I would die before I hurt her.

Will you promise?

She nods. "Yes, I promise. But not for THEM. I'll do it for you. Because I love you."

With that – and a gentle touch of my jaw, which is hanging slack – she rises, and sweeps off to her room, closing the door quietly behind her. I know she needs the time, so I leave and am taken back to my own floor. My own world. It is so empty, so meaningless without her. I find no comfort or pleasure in the things I used to love. Even my Parker-Hale; even my Glock. Against her, every endeavour seems futile and hollow.

Inside me I am empty too; but it is an emptiness borne of freedom and brings calm where before I would feel lost. Max has gone, maybe to the hunting ground of Heaven where all lions catch their prey. Jeremiah – praise the Lord – will never come back; I scared him away, he has found a better place to be. It is just me and her. And now that she has gone, it is just me.

Just me. Alone. It has not been this way in a long, long while.

Having glimpsed her childhood, I start thinking of my own. A dim and ill-remembered – maybe fabled – time, swamped in mists three decades of others' lives have hidden carefully, and well.

I still have the photographs, though, and a moment's search unearths them all; I sit beneath a dim light and look back at a past I have learned a thousand times over how to bury and forget.

The pictures are in black and white, faded grey with age. They are not arranged in albums – there are too few. They are not in any sense of order, but scattered like fragments of ash and enclosed in an envelope that can be carried in the pocket or at the bottom of a suitcase, or in the sole of a shoe, where they are safest kept from curious eyes. In Geneva, I had my shoes taken from me, so I kept the photos in my boxers. No-one thought to look in there.

I was a boy, once, the photographs attest. A small boy, with short, dark, unruly hair, like rich brown soil churned up by a trowel. I had light eyes that caught the sun and sometimes turned a little hazel; they smiled, those eyes, but I have forgotten why, and I have not seen that smile in them for the longest time. They saw and looked and never judged, but smiled the smile of a peaceful soul.

I was a loved child, a protected child. I had freckles from summer days spend scooping tadpoles in the pond behind the house, and scratches on my arms from rooting in blackberry bushes, trying to catch the cat.

The house was old grey stone, cold in winter but for the hearty fires; cool in summer. But my favourite place was the bottom of the garden, where overgrown thickets revealed to a curious child the wonders of a hidden world, tucked away from adult eyes, where I would play alone, content.

I would sit beneath the hedges, in a pocket of the world where no hand ever plunged; and in all the hours I spent there I imagined many ways my life would be.

But never the way it became.

I have no photos of my father, but I remember a tall, straight-legged man in brown suit trousers, wearing a patient smile beneath the brightness of his brilliant eyes.

I can remember the times he searched the garden for me, calling out my name, telling the me he could not see the wonderful things my mother had made for me to eat, and knowing all the while exactly where I was, and smiling when I crawled out into the sunshine and ran to hug his legs.

He read to me at dinnertime, as I sat with plate-wide eyes beside my mother and chewed her noisy offerings; we listened to his voice, she and I, and the expressions on his face, the music of his laughter, I shall always remember, though I may never call to mind the words he spoke, as with mere words he transported us a thousand miles away.

My mother was a figure of my life I recall with greater tactility; the plump softness of her embrace, the nimble caring of her hands. She grew things in our garden, and I ate of these delicious labours as they were presented to me; jam and pies, baked apples and blackberry crumble.

She brushed my teeth and washed my face and sang me lullabies, the words to which I have forgotten, if I ever knew them at all. Mostly I think I listened to her voice, that gentle sea that rocked me to sleep and washed away my troubles and my tears.

I could have been six when all this changed. When, after a long day of play, I took refuge from the hot sun beneath a hedge, and fell asleep. Cool air touched my skin when I woke, and the bright sun had faded to early evening shade.

I waited, as I always did, for my father to come home and find me out, and talk to me as he pretended to search the garden, never checking in the one place where I always hid, so that it would always be my sanctum.

I waited for an age – for that is what an hour or two seems like to a child, whose day is short with lengthy sleep and made quick with youthful energy – but he did not come. I waited and I waited, until I heard my mother calling from the house, and heard a note in her voice I could not name, but which struck in me a chord of fear.

I fled the hiding place and ran to her, and found in her tight embrace a shudder that made the foundations of my happy childhood tremble.

Soon after that day, after my father did not come to find me, the luxuries I had come to know as ordinary disappeared. Frost and cold stole away the garden, I found no joy in treading the crisp white grass; the fallen leaves and twigs cut my shoeless feet, the bitter air nipped my skin and drove me back inside, though inside was little warmer. The fire always blazed too low in the hearth, many a time it guttered and died, and all my shivering and pleas could not bring it back.

With the coming of winter, my mother's soft embraces disappeared. She grew thin and weak, and I was too small to understand why. Food was scarce, warmth a thing of memory, joy a distant torment to my soul. I tried and tried to make my mother smile and eat, but before the coming of spring she slipped away; my mother died in her bed, lonely and alone despite my clinging to her hand. My father's disappearance was never explained, and no-one but my mother and I seemed to miss him. If my mother knew the reason for his leaving, she took it with her to her grave.

I clutch the photograph in a hand that trembles and stare, only a moment, at the picture it portrays; husband, wife and son, smiling and content. The last picture that remains, the last scrap of evidence of our happy existence.

To this day I don't know where my father went, or who he was, or what he did, or why he left my mother and I, or didn't come back to suffer stoically at her funeral.

The very few photos taken after that time are sterile; I passed into a foster home, then another, and another, with no real memory of myself or my own life. I shut my heart and soul away inside a body that felt strange and numb. I let the world pass over me; I had nothing to give to it, and I had been deprived of all I could want.

Those days were dark and without hope, joy, warmth or love. Perhaps that is why I look back on them so infrequently, and why I have tried so hard since to bury my early memories beneath a collage of other people's lives.

Those times are what made Max so strong in me; they are the reason I am strong. Because I have had to be.

I clutch the memory in my hand, and crush it. It crumples, weak as paper, and I release it to the floor. It doesn't matter now who finds it. By the time they realise it was me, I shall be gone from this place.

The realisation of what I must do should bring fear to my chest, but instead I feel strangely calm. The heart that beats my blood is pumping softly, quietly, coolly; it is a hushing rhythm, like the sound the wind makes through the acacia trees in the park, when I am the only one who hears it.

I put the photographs down on the bed. I should not have kept them when I began my work for THEM, and if THEY knew I had them now I would be dead. I have done many things THEY would disapprove of; I have kept scraps of myself, I have stored pictures and notes of The Targets in The Mission Files, and all these things would be THEIR downfall if they were discovered.

I think, though it may be my undoing, that it is time THEY *were* discovered.

Final Mission

I made The Call. I made The Call at *precisely* twenty-seven minutes past three this afternoon, talking as THEY listened in silence to my words.

My very…deliberate…words.

I had prepared these words and run them over in my head for a long time before dialling The Number and making The Call and telling THEM *exactly* what THEY wanted to hear.

Mission 66 has been cancelled. There will be no more Missions.

I have always known I was expendable to THEM. Useful, pliable and obedient for sixty-five Missions; an absolute asset to the smooth functioning of the system; invaluable and essential – until I am no longer needed, when I am cast aside and severed from the line that has kept my heart beating, filled my lungs and paid my bills for sixty-five Missions.

I know THEY will come for me. I knew this before I made The Call. I have always known this.

THEY will come here and break down the door, and shoot me with their guns. THEY will expect me to die, and perhaps I shall.

But I shall not die without a fight.

I have set it up.

She is gone. She is gone, and won't return – I made her promise not to come back. THEY can't hurt her now.

118

If I die tonight, I die with the knowledge that she is safe. I die a good death, a happy death. Knowing that I have had a taste of Heaven, and have left Heaven safe and unspoiled in my wake.

~

THEY don't know I am waiting for THEM. THEY are creeping quietly up the stairs, guns cocked and raised and silenced.

My apartment is dark, but the light from the hallway seeps under the door a little way, and I see THEIR shoes outside, casting shadows in the slot of light.

The Glock is silent in my hands. Its warm weight reassures me, as it has reassured me a thousand times before, in the same manner as my kettle, but more *reliable*. I feel a surge of hatred that the kettle gave in to Death and abandoned me when I needed it the most.

I focus the hatred where it is needed – towards THEM.

THEY open the door – which I locked and bolted – with ease, and slip inside.

THEY leave the lights off as they sweep each room, working as one creature, though there are two of THEM – the same two, I am willing to bet, who jumped me in the park and hit my head with a crowbar. I feel the hatred rise again.

Good. Anger is good.

THEY spread out, one branching off to search my bedroom and the other coming closer to my hiding place. THEY aren't *really* expecting me to be here (who waits for Death, knowing He will come?) but THEY must sweep the location nonetheless. THEY will find my photographs, my shopping lists, my books; THEY will destroy them, burn the apartment. I have already removed everything of value to me. I have removed The Mission Files. Everything else can burn.

This one is very close to me now. He is poking around in the cushions of the sofa where we sat together, she and I, only I have since turned it from the window and moved it up against the wall, to give myself a place to hide. Now I kneel behind it, Glock clasped in both hands. I feel like praying – not because I am in any way religious, nor because I feel I need to, but just because I am already in the position for it.

He is so close to me that I can read his shoes around the side of the sofa; they are the same shoes I saw as the park rushed up and hit me in the face so many nights ago. I smile grimly to myself in the darkness. Revenge is a dish best served behind the sofa, with a loaded gun.

I push the Glock up above the cushions, and fire twice.

The sound of the silenced pistol is like the sudden release of compressed gas – CO_2, perhaps, from a bottle of Jacob's Creek Chardonnay – but the resulting sound is far more rewarding. A wet squelch, and a *thud* as he hits the floor. He didn't even have time for a death cry.

But his friend heard the *thud* and rushes back, gun at the ready, just as I leap away from the body and run for the kitchen door. The silenced shots follow me – *poft, poft, poft* – and the bullets embed themselves in the wall in sprays of plaster.

The man curses and follows swiftly, waiting just outside the kitchen. He fires blindly into the small room; denting the fridge, splintering the cupboard doors, cracking the tiles.

He misses me entirely, but I can see his black-gloved hand as it wields the gun that wants me dead. I take aim at that glove the next time it appears, and put a hole straight through his palm.

He yells and drops the gun, stumbling away from the wall into the darkness of the living room and making for the door.

I rise and run after him (realising, with a twinge and a gasp, that he did not miss *entirely*) and tackle him to the ground.

He has a second gun now and takes aim, but I thump it aside and kick his hand until he drops it. It spins away and is snagged and stopped by carpet.

Now he has a knife (where *does* he pull these weapons from?) and he slashes at me with it, scrambling to his feet. I raise an arm in defence and get it cut, but bash him backwards against the wall. He lashes out once again, and loses his blade in my shoulder.

Too furious to register the pain, I slam him into the wall again and drag him back into the living room, throwing him to the floor and pinning him there with my boot on his chest and the Glock's elongated muzzle pointed roundly at his head.

No more stupid manoeuvres, I tell him, gritting my teeth – not against the pain, for there will be little of that until the adrenaline clears, but against the knowledge that the pain will come, and against the curious numbness in my shoulder where the blade is lodged, and in my back where a bullet now resides. *You work for THEM?* I ask.

He sneers in silence.

I remove the gun from his head and point it instead between his legs. The colour drains like dishwater from his face.

I say, *I have absolutely no compunction about shooting your balls off. But I may let you die a man, if you tell me what I want to hear.*

He considers this, sweat glistening on his face in the semi-dark. Eventually he nods.

Good. You work for THEM? I ask again.

Nod, nod, nod.

I waggle the gun above his family jewels. *So? Tell me.*

He swallows nervously. "THEY told us just to warn you. In the park, the other night…"

Yes, I remember. Get on with it.

122

"THEY think...you're a liability now. Even before you met the girl, THEY wanted rid of you, but THEY wanted to make it seem...like suicide. THEY knew you'd go to the girl..."

How? How did they know?

"You fit the profile, don't you? THEY chose you because THEY knew THEY could control you. THEY knew you'd go to the girl when you were hurt, then you'd have to find a way of getting rid of her because she knew too much about you. Sooner or later she would ask questions. THEY gave you the perfect opportunity, setting up Mission 66. THEY wanted *you* to kill her."

Me. Not Jeremiah, not even Max, but *me. Why?*

Then the truth, the odourless drug, seeps into my brain.

THEY wanted me to kill her, because... I look at the painting on the wall, the hideous Hiroshima that masked the bullet hole of my darkest hours. Those hours had followed Jennifer's death, when all I could see was her pale face and her wide eyes, and the mouth that frame the deepest grief imaginable.

I had tried to shoot myself, in the aftermath of that Mission, but I had missed.

"Your profile fit. Everything fit. After you'd shot the girl, THEY knew you'd shoot yourself."

History repeats itself, I muttered, and swung the gun back up to his head.

The adrenaline was fading, and the beating of my heart echoed around the bullet and reverberated along the knife-blade. My hands would shake soon, my vision blur and my strength fail as my blood soaked away. I tightened my grip on the trigger.

There's one thing THEY overlooked, I told him, as he stared along the barrel at his death. *When Niall…when* I *shot Jennifer, and came back here, and tried to shoot myself…*

I feel my legs begin to buckle and remove my foot from his chest. I keep the Glock trained at his head, and slowly, painfully kneel down beside him.

I missed on purpose, *don't you see? Suicide's the easy way out. I took The Shot and missed on purpose.*

I am not Ned today; I had a home once, and parents who loved me.

I am not Robert; I could never fathom maths, but I knew how to *live.*

I am not Gerald; my dreams were more humble than going to the moon.

I am not Jack; I knew once how to laugh and play, but learned that life was serious, too.

I am not Eric; I *have* chopped wood – my father showed me how when I was a boy.

I am not Harry; I had a dog, not a hamster. A lovely retriever called Bonnie.

I am not Jeremiah. The Lord owes me nothing, and I am at His whim. I am but a speck in the grand scheme of things, though I like to think I've made a difference.

I am not Max. I hunt to eat, I hunt to survive – I do not hunt for sport.

It seems THEY don't have me figured out quite yet. I'm only realising it myself, but I don't fit the profile. I squeeze the trigger, and put another hole in her ceiling.

I guess I'll have to create a profile of my own.

0: Back to the Beginning

I staggered onto the street under cover of the night, and found my way to the park. This is the place where my life began, I'm sure of it. Bleeding to death in this park, this is where I made the choice that led me to her.

I sank to my knees in the grass and watched, consciousness ebbing away, as flames licked my apartment into light and devoured everything I once called mine. Oddly, I felt no sadness. What was up there, anyway, besides a collection of objects that belonged to all the different people I'd ever tried to be? All the possessions in the world could not make me *me* – I am what I carry around inside myself, and what I like to be the most, and what *she* found in me.

I grip the blades of grass beneath my knees with weak, useless fingers, and imagine I see the old man's face at the window, smiling at last.

No matter what happens to me now, I think, *at least I know she's safe.*

But how I miss her.

Suddenly, she is here. She is pulling me towards her and cradling me against her body. Her arms are strong, so strong, and I feel like they could save me from the world. Her tears damp my hair as she cries helplessly over the blood that soaks my clothes. She has broken her promise and come back for me, but I can't feel angry at her. I love her too much.

I try to speak, but she can't make out the words above the sound of the fire and the rising wail of sirens. She leans in closer.

"I don't...even know...your name," I whisper, and find my voice at last.

"Shh, shh," she murmurs, holding my hands. It feels as if she is rocking me gently, although it could be the bullet in me, and the blood that *should* be in me, but is seeping slowly out. Blood and bullets have always had a way of rocking me.

"THEY...THEM," I try to say, but the words are pushed back inside me. I can barely draw breath now and I wonder where that bullet went. "THEY...are finished," I manage.

Her breaths cover my head with warm and cold, warm and cold. My body is growing cold, but the slick surface of my skin feels warm, and though her body against mine is warm too, her hands, holding mine, are cold. Warm and cold, warm and cold. I look up into her face when she does not reply and see it there too; warm and cold, warm and cold.

Warmth in her smile; coldness in her eyes.

"What do you mean?" she asks. "THEY are..."

"Finished...done..." I whisper, and see the subtle change of her expression. One of her hands leaves mine; the other, delicate and cold, is gripping both of mine, pinning them in place.

"What did you do with The Files?" she asks. Her hand tightens around mine, and not for the first time I am powerless to resist her. But I don't want to, anyway.

"I sent them…away…to someone…who will know…what to do…"

"Tell me who. Who did you send them to?"

"A very…nice…policeman…"

I am fighting to breathe, now, and the night is closing in. The fire is a fading, failing light, but I can see everything so much clearer. If there is a light at the end of the tunnel, it is shining into every dark corner of my life and all the shadows are disappearing. Finally, finally, finally I understand.

"I'm…Dave," I tell her, with surprising ease. Why has this taken me so long to say?

"I know," she whispers. Her eyes are cold no more; the beautiful girl downstairs is back, holding me in her arms. I can feel the movement of the hand she took away; I know what she is doing, what she is reaching for, and I am completely unafraid; perhaps because I know it is inevitable, or perhaps because I would prefer to go no other way.

"Can I just…know your name?"

She does not have to think so long before replying; she knows there is no harm in telling me, now. Her voice is like warm water, like the tender skin of a brimming bath as I let my head sink under and feel the tiny ripples lap over my eyes.

"Mae," she answers at last, stroking my face with the silver barrel of the gun. A Sig Sauer 229. I used one for a while, back in '82. I wonder how many times she has used this before, on who, and where, and why.

I wonder why I never, never, never saw this coming. Maybe I just didn't want to.

The pain becomes mere background noise. All I can feel is her skin against mine, my hands grasped in hers, her breasts against my head. *They're so soft.*

It was good while it lasted, honestly. While it lasted, it was the best time of my life.

"I'm sorry…about…your ceiling," I murmur.

"I'm not," she says, softly, and smiles, and cocks the gun.

I say, "I'm glad it was you," and think, *not the greatest epitaph,* and close my eyes.

~

What do birds *do*, when they sit on the apex of a roof, neck stretched, body still and erect, wings drawn back and tucked away, when they look for all the world like gallant storybook heroes in a favourite hero pose? Do they think about their lives? All the beautiful places they have been? Do they muse sadly about all the friends and loved ones they have known and lost?

Or do they perhaps look to the horizon, that far-off unknown, where the sun sets before they can chase it and rises before they can flee, and wonder what lies beyond?

And when they launch themselves from that high pinnacle, and seem to fall towards their deaths, do they contemplate that death? Do they wish to end their short lives the sooner, in order that no more of their friends and loved ones should pass away before their eyes? And when at last they spread their wings and let the wind take them up, up, up, away from concrete oblivion, do they think what might have been, or set their beaks in resolution that those beautiful, faraway places should never escape them again?

Do they soar towards that lost horizon, certain in the knowledge that they will chase the sun to its death and find a new world beyond, or die in trying?

I am that bird, that lustful pigeon, that dark crow, that solitary robin, that swift and nimble sparrow. I am that graceful, sail-winged swan. I see the horizon stretched out before me, and I long for it. I long to feel the sun burn the glue from my feathers; I long to see the Earth spiral up towards me, promising to hit me in the face.

I long for the freedom to choose whether or not to pull the cord and open the parachute, or to simply close my eyes and let the gentle wind take me where it will.

www.lefryerstokes.com

Printed in Great Britain
by Amazon